PENGUIN BOOKS

THE PROFESSIONAL

Ashok Ferrey is the author of five books, four of them nominated for the Gratiaen Prize and the fifth for the State Literary Award. By day he is a personal trainer.

The Professional

ASHOK FERREY

PENGUIN BOOKS

PENGUIN BOOKS

USA | Canada | UK | Ireland | Australia
New Zealand | India | South Africa | China

Penguin Books is part of the Penguin Random House group of companies
whose addresses can be found at global.penguinrandomhouse.com

Published by Penguin Random House India Pvt. Ltd
7th Floor, Infinity Tower C, DLF Cyber City,
Gurgaon 122 002, Haryana, India

First published in Vintage by Random House India 2013
Published in Penguin Books by Penguin Random House India 2017

Copyright © Ashok Ferrey 2013

ISBN 9780143440154

For sale in the Indian Subcontinent only

Typeset in Melior by R. Ajith Kumar
Printed at Replika Press Pvt. Ltd, India

www.penguin.co.in

For Amantha Helena

1

Chamath opened his eyes. From his sleeping bag on the floor he looked up through the window at the sky above, a great square of blinding white light flickering like a blank TV screen. It could go either way: to the velvety black of a thunderstorm or the scorching blue of high summer; it was that sort of day.

He closed his eyes. The blank white light flooded his entire body, flowing through to the ends of his fingers and toes—and he was suffused with a happiness only the young can feel. At twenty-two he was of an age when anything is possible; and nothing is possible.

He spread his arms out in the crucifix position. He felt through his fingers the rough softness of the pine floorboards, every bump and ridge, every groove of the timber, and his mind tingled with the knowledge that he was strapped securely to the earth, while at the same time hurtling through the great white blankness of the sky.

Through the gaps in the floorboards he could hear Jamila padding about in the flat below, softly because she knew he'd be still asleep. He could picture her with her wiry red headdress of hair, stooping slightly—the fluffy white robe barely reaching the tops of her over-long brown legs in their furry bedroom slippers—looking like a particularly beautiful species of immigrant stork. This image raised endless possibilities. Sighing, because at the same time there was absolutely no promise of fulfilment, he went to the loo where he peed with difficulty. Opening the door to his flat he went downstairs to the front door to pick up his single pint of Silver Top. The door to the ground-floor flat opened and Jamila came out.

'Rough night?'

'Not rough enough,' he replied looking at her.

Jamila and he had what could only be described as a working relationship: sometimes it worked, sometimes it didn't. Last night they had watched a video together. At about ten she had said for no reason at all, 'Right, off you go then.'

'But it's early,' he stammered.

'Exactly. I want an early night.'

Jamila worked in a charity shop on the other side of London; she didn't have to go in till mid-morning. On occasion, coming back late he could hear her moving about downstairs. Every tap, every bump was an invitation: *Come and get me, I'm still up.* But he

2

never did. Not that he didn't want to. Just. Because at twenty-two anything is possible; even though nothing is possible.

'I collected your mail,' she said handing him three envelopes. A red-letter gas bill, a red-letter electricity bill. And a thin blue aerogramme with his name and address typewritten on the front. He recognized the work of his father's Olivetti Portable, with its smudged script and its e with the centre missing that looked like an o.

'Thanks,' he said and went back up.

My dear boy,

This is not an easy letter to write, but write it I must. Whatever you think of me once you have finished, please remember that I am your father, and that I will always love you. As you know life was never easy for us but we managed somehow. You are now the proud possessor of a Maths degree from probably the finest university in the world. Any door anywhere in the world will open for you if you just utter the magic word *Oxford*.

With those last funds I sent you, you will by now have finished carpeting the flat. If there is anything left over please use it to buy curtains. By the end of next month, at the very latest, we need to get some tenants in. I leave all this in your capable hands. All I can do is to inform you that from next month the mortgage is *your* responsibility, that I no longer have the financial resources to support you overseas. I hope and pray that a decent job will get you the work permit you so desire, that with your salary you will be able to find a room, and have enough left over to keep body and soul together. The rent from the flat will barely cover the mortgage payments and that is why a tenant is so necessary. *This is what you must not fall behind on.* Anyway, you are the Maths graduate not me; I don't need to tell you anything about finances. If all else fails, you know what to do. There is always a home for you here, and you know it is not a bad one. Be well, dear boy, and be good.

    Lovingly,

Your Appachi

PS—Always remember who you are, where you have come from.

It could all have been said in one sentence: *You're on your own now, mate.*

Chamath felt like a dumb animal who's been hit in the hindquarters for no reason. He thought: Why are you doing this to me? He folded the letter and put it in his pocket. Today was Sunday, his one free day from the site, and he drifted aimlessly up Hiley Road, blown this way and that like a scrap of paper in the wind. It was what he liked doing best, submerging himself in this random inner city life. There was something bleak and comfortless about Kensal Green on Sunday—its skip-laden, wind-blown streets. Many houses were boarded up, and hardly any sound came from ones which were occupied: it was as if the giant machinery that ran the city had ground to a halt on this seventh day, the day of its rest. The only desultory signs of life came from the few immigrant shops of the neighbourhood: Mr Shafeeq at the corner, newly arrived from Uganda, always good for a twenty-minute chat about Idi Amin; and next door to him, the young Aussie couple who had just opened an organic fruit shop. (Those green papayas, he wanted to say, will never ripen. I'm afraid they weren't properly *pahila* when plucked. They're only good for currying. Or you could shred them, deep fry, and dress them in a salad. Of course he didn't say all this because it would have broken their young organic hearts.) Then there was the library at the corner of Bathurst Gardens: his very own oasis at the heart of this polyglot souk of small-time immigrants. Roll on Monday, he thought, when life would return to normal with the grind and crunch of the machinery's enormous cog wheels.

He thought of the unpaid red-letter bills, and the carpet money which had unaccountably slipped through his fingers. Where had it all gone? And so quickly too. He thought of the other option open to him. I will not go back, he thought defiantly. *I would rather die.*

Hippodrome Mews was a prize-winning development; at least that was the first thing they told you when you went there. Each tiny house had a kitchen-diner as you entered, two bedrooms up a spiral iron staircase, and right at the top on the second floor, a sitting-room with sliding glass doors to a small terrace.

Chamath could see that it was a design that would never work back home in Sri Lanka. Your kids asleep on the middle floor while your party guests clanked up and down the staircase from kitchen to roof-top? Perhaps these houses were not designed for married couples. Perhaps marriage and kids were the last things on a Londoner's mind if he lived in Hippodrome Mews. He realized he had a lot to learn about this big city life.

Jonas and he were the new kids on site.

'You have your national insurance number?' they were asked the day they were hired.

'*Of course,*' said Jonas. Chamath was silent. Neither he nor Jonas was legal. This didn't seem to worry management and both were signed up. *Oxford* may be a magic word, Chamath thought wryly; it didn't open doors if you didn't have a work permit. And on a building site they'd surely drive you out if they knew you had anything as ridiculous as a university degree. He kept very quiet about all this though his plummy accent raised a few suspicious looks before he learned to tone it down.

Their first job was to unload a lorry full of cement bags.

Jonas looked critically at Chamath's legs. 'You think those chicken legs can manage these hundredweight bags?'

'Just watch me,' Chamath said boldly.

The lorry was backed up to the edge of a deep trench across which was a nine-inch scaffold board. They would have to carry each bag across the trench, wobbling along the board, to dump it in the stores. Chamath had never carried such heavy weights before, and not across what looked like a murderous ravine. If you fell you would probably break a leg. He knew better than to think too much about it. That was how it was. You were strapped securely to the system, hurtling off into the blank white unknown. There was no room for doubt. Only an unshakeable faith in a status quo which might let you down only if you were fool enough to stop and think about it.

Fifty cement bags later his legs and thighs felt like iron.

'Man, I can never get over you Sri Lankans,' said Jonas shaking his head admiringly. 'Are you all like this?'

Chamath grinned. 'Like what?' he asked innocently.

'You don't complain. You don't protest. You just get on with it even if it kills you. I'd say you were the bravest race on earth, if I didn't know you were actually the stupidest!'

Chamath punched him playfully in the chest as they crossed the road to the park opposite, where they sat on a bench to share their lunchtime sandwiches. There were young mothers with kids in the playground. Not your average Hippodrome Mews residents then, Chamath thought.

From where they were sitting they could see two men in grey suits, one tall one short, going into the site office.

'Buyers,' said Chamath.

Jonas shook his head. 'Surveyors, I think.'

'Maybe they're from Immigration.'

Jonas looked at him for a moment, sternly. 'You don't joke about that sort of thing, man. If they come, run. Run like the wind.'

The sandwiches were from the pub round the corner, cheese and pickle, and roast beef. They broke them in two, shared them out and began to eat. There was an unearthly shriek behind them. One of the kids had taken a tumble off the swing. She saw them watching, picked herself up, and got straight back on as if nothing had happened. They turned back to their lunch and the grey suits were standing in front of them.

Chamath's blood ran cold.

'Mr Williams? Mr Pili. . . er. . .Pilima?'

'What's it to you?' asked Jonas.

The tall man had gaunt over-shaved blue cheeks. He stood uneasily in his suit, like a sort of off-duty monk in mufti. Ignoring their hostility he handed each of them a card. *Embassy Services*, Chamath read. *Your pleasure. Our duty*. There was a central London address and two telephone numbers.

'Would either of you lads be interested in some work after hours? Bit of dosh on the side?'

'Do we look that desperate?'

The man put out his palms as if to ward off this attack. 'I didn't say that. It's just . . .' He looked at the two of them and sighed. 'I can see you two could make a fortune. Bright lads like you.'

'What's it involve?'

'If you're *really* interested,' he said with a pained expression, 'give us a call.'

'Oh, it's nothing illegal,' the other man cut in. This one had thinning sandy hair, and very pale grey eyes that looked out at the world with a permanent look of hurt. 'We wouldn't be involved in anything illegal, would we, Mike?'

'I didn't see you offering anyone else a job,' Jonas said belligerently.

The tall man looked over towards the site and shook his head reluctantly. 'Not many are called,' he said sadly. 'Even fewer are chosen.'

'You're not serious!' Chamath said as they walked home.

'Why not?' Jonas was quiet for a moment. He looked at his friend speculatively. 'Some of us,' he said after a while, 'are not too proud to take up kind offers when they come our way. They said it was nothing illegal.' They walked the rest of the way in silence.

Back home Chamath wandered round his bare, empty flat, devoid of music or books or pictures. None of that seemed even slightly necessary. There was him, there was the earth, and nothing in-between; and he felt all-powerful. All the same when Jamila popped her head round the door and said, 'I'm cooking stew tonight,' he didn't say no. Jamila's stews were legendary. It never did to enquire too closely what went into them because quite frequently Jamila herself had forgotten by the time they were ready to eat. Today it was goat and spinach, and a quarter bottle of Lea and Perrins, and a quarter bottle of Tabasco. But it could just as easily have been fish head and okra, and a quarter bottle of Lea and Perrins and a quarter bottle of Tabasco. The only constants were the sauces. Sometimes you felt she was singlehandedly keeping all the sauce-bottling plants in the country afloat.

He looked around her flat, at the curtains with their oversize blue roses, the clashing yellow tribal-print rug: the apparent randomness of it all. He envied her the singularity of her style, her sublime indifference to the ghastly good taste of the English. It occurred to him that her life was made up of these simple strong events, the undisputed constants of her life. It allowed her to face her problems head-on, armed with an abbreviated and simplified vocabulary of rights and wrongs that informed her code of ethics. He thought with a certain weariness of the sinuous curves, the almost Byzantine complexity of his own Asian morality. It was probably the reason he liked to keep his flat bare and raw: to counteract the weight of this burdensome sophistication. It was definitely the reason he didn't want to go back home to Sri Lanka.

They shared the stew on the sofa watching a video, and afterwards, with a matter-of-factness that took his breath away, she peeled off her top and let him nuzzle her glossy brown nipples; and when she was ready she arched her back to put a cushion underneath, putting him in at the same time.

It was the cleanest sex he'd had in a long time. *How much dirtier it could be*, he thought regretfully. *If only she'd let me!*

The old man stopped typing and looked out of his window at Galle Road, the busiest road in Sri Lanka. He found to his surprise he had grown hard. You ought to be ashamed of yourself, he thought, at your age. Guiltily he put a hand down to cover his lap, but there was no danger of anyone coming up the stairs. He could hear music from below. They were at it again. Victor Sylvester.

The old man was inordinately fond of his typewriter, an Olympia #27-882402. It was electric, and in mint condition. There was absolutely no question of its es looking like os. It had caused problems when he first lugged it into the house.

'Electric?' asked Barbara. 'Oh. Does it consume much?'

The old man honestly didn't know.

'We might have to charge you a teensy weensy bit extra,' said Ginnie.

Barbara and Ginevra. His landladies. On most matters they thought and spoke alike; though in looks they could not have been more different. Ginnie the elder carried the day—with her languid limbs, her commanding height. But seasoned shopper that he was, the old man firmly averted his eyes from the precise commodity he might desire for fear of pushing up its price. Instead he treated the two sisters with strict equality—as if they were a sort of two-headed landlady—deferring if at all to the younger one, Bar, small of stature with hardened coal-black eyes.

In the end they charged him 1,500 rupees for electricity, bringing his total rent to 18,500 a month, which was really not bad, he thought, not for the middle of Colombo anyway. For this he got a room over the garage, a tiny lavatory with the lid permanently off the cistern (to flush, you plunged your hand into the rusting water and pulled up whatever came to hand) and a small two-burner tabletop stove which occupied the entrance corridor. One of the burners had disintegrated with rust. Down two steps from the dining room ('Not many flats, dear, can boast of a separate dining room') was the living area, with his bed pushed against one window, and his desk against the other. It wasn't much, but it was enough. Though he always looked grumpy the old man was supremely happy. As long as he could click-clack away on his typewriter he was content.

Though he didn't realize it, he was the cause of endless speculation downstairs. Why exactly was he here? The land-ladies were torn. On the one hand, though they had boundless faith in the unparalleled quality of their accommodation, they knew in their hearts that 18,500 was daylight robbery. Either their lodger was extremely clever or an absolute idiot.

'He's from the Inland Revenue,' said Bar decisively. 'He's here to investigate Daddy's millions.'

'Daddy left us virtually nothing when he died.'

'But he's not to know that,' said Bar cunningly.

Then there was the very vexing question of his typing, to be heard at all hours of the day and night, clickety-clack, clickety-clack.

'Maybe it's the income tax report,' said Ginnie.

'Already?'

'He's obviously a quick worker.'

'I think he's after one of us,' decided Bar.

At this the ladies felt a pleasurable little frisson of fear. But was he after you (Bar) or me (Ginnie)?

Or do you think, my dear, that he's gay?

This last question was the most interesting of all. The landladies had only just learnt the new meaning of the word. Brought up in 50s Colombo where parties were gay and frocks were gay and even cars could sometimes be gay, they couldn't get over the concept of a lodger who was grumpy as well as gay. As well as working for the Income Tax.

'I think he's after you, Gin. I see the way he looks at you.'

'Nonsense, Bar. He's always been partial to small girls. He told me.'

'Told you? *Told you?* When? Have you been chatting to him behind my back? Oh, you cheeky monkey, you're having me on, aren't you!'

The old man loved to watch the traffic while he typed: two endless metallic gear chains grinding slowly in opposite directions. His windows faced the junction of Shrubbery Gardens and Galle Road, and the traffic never stopped. Every day he could hear it long before he awoke, rumbling through his sleeping body as if he were strapped to the rails in the way of an oncoming goods train. Sometimes at three in the morning he awoke to silence. And then he could hear that other sound, deeper, more menacing than the traffic: the growl of the sea.

The old man looked around his sparsely furnished bedsit. It had a bareness that pleased him tremendously. He had to change the newspaper under the leaking Sisil fridge every day: by morning it was a pulpy mess of wet paper, a satisfactory end to yesterday's news. In the cupboard above there were two tins of peaches, his one guilty indulgence. He rationed himself to one tin a week. Inside the fridge were chicken legs individually wrapped, and slices of Keells ham. The old man had always loved his food; once upon a time he had been quite good at cooking, but had got out of the habit because for much of his life there had been people around him who took pity on him and fed him. He raised his head, and the long-ago smell of curry goat and spinach filled his nostrils, sharp and vinegary. There was a sudden vicious stab of pain in his stomach—acutely physical, visceral—and he felt a gush of liquid inside as if he were bleeding internally. The body remembers, he thought grimly. Even if the mind has so faithlessly forgotten.

Downstairs they had pushed the chairs back to create a space in the middle. It wasn't really enough. Two steps in one direction and you were at the front door, almost, with its pretty art deco grillwork. Two steps back and you bumped into the Sacred Heart picture hanging on the wall. And if you were really careless and upset the little red glass lamp underneath, you ended up with hot wax all over your dress.

'Well, what's it to be?'

'Why do you ask, Bar? You *know* you always put on the Victor Sylvester.'

Barbara put on the Victor Sylvester.

'I'll lead then, shall I?'

'Oh, Bar, you're always leading. If only you could see how ridiculous it looks. You're a head shorter!'

'Now don't start that business again, Ginnie dear. You know I can't help it if I've gone like Mummy.'

'Well be careful then, and don't back me into the Sacred Heart. Sometimes I think you do it on purpose.'

They danced for a while in silence.

'I really think we should go upstairs and ask Him to join us, don't you?'

'He doesn't look the dancing type to *me*, dear.'

'Well you know what they say. It's a vertical expression of a horizontal desire.'

'What is?'

'Oh, don't be dim, Bar. *You* know.'

'But I thought we had agreed that he was an unmitigated virgin?'

The music suddenly stopped and the word *virgin* hung in the air, loud and clear. The landladies froze guiltily, expecting the old man to come charging downstairs to refute all allegations. But there was only silence from above.

2

Chamath's mother had died when he was five. The only memory that remained was of a white blouse against which his face was pressed. Not so much a memory as a smell: the smell of some vague abstract essence of motherhood he could barely recreate in his mind, so that he wondered at times whether it was just the idea of the smell that was hardwired into his brain, a false positive of all the love and comfort and care that might have been if only his mother had lived.

His father had brought him up to the best of his ability, this only child. You might have thought that because there were just the two of them they would have become brothers in arms, or best buddies. Instead they were like two old gentlemen in a train carriage, civil and sanguine, courteous and shy with each other. So much was assumed, so much left unsaid: sometimes Chamath longed to reach out and shake his father, if only to get a rise out of him. Years later he would come to realize that it was this lack of emotional love that put him permanently on the lookout for a mother, a father, a brother or sister in every friend he made, accommodating himself to their every whim and fancy in a touching and almost childlike desire to please.

'Oh man,' said Jonas disparagingly. 'You're just like water. You'll take the shape of any cup you're put into.'

But it had not been an unhappy childhood. Every so often he dreamt of it, and in his dreams he was that child again with the bow-legged walk, wandering through an evergreen maze that smelt sharp and fresh in the sunlight. And in the dream he could put his hand right up to touch the top, smooth yet prickly, and he knew with a sort of sweet sadness, and a knowledge which belied his years—this was a dream after all— that there was no way out: it was his lot to live in this maze forever, to appease and please whichever monster happened to be lurking around the corner.

Hippodrome Mews was at the wrong end of Ladbroke Grove, in an area the estate agents liked to call 'North Kensington'. There were thirteen houses in all, in various stages of construction, the ones at the start painted and almost complete, the ones at the end still gaunt skeletons of metal and timber. The whole area was like the site of some vast Napoleonic battle, with squadrons of plasterers, electricians and bricklayers all walking in formation in apparently random directions. Being the lowest in the food chain Chamath knew very few people, and even fewer who made the effort to smile or say *Wotcher mate!* There was no sign of Jonas when he went into the site office to sign on.

'They've been asking for your national insurance number again,' said Val. Val was site foreman—skinny, dark and Irish—the Napoleon of the building site. The rolling rs of his accent sounded kind to Chamath's ears, and he always smiled when he spoke to the new boys.

'You know what this is?' Val held up a caulking gun. He showed him how to load a canister of silicone, cutting off the top; he took him over to the first house in the street, the most complete.

'We'll start at the top,' he said. He showed Chamath how to squeeze silicone around the glass in the window frames—not too firm, not too gentle—licking your finger afterwards and running it along the wet silicone to firm it into place before it hardened. It was the laziest work imaginable, but it beat unloading cement. At lunchtime he met Jonas.

'I phoned them,' Jonas said.

'Who?'

'Embassy Services. They want us to come in Sunday morning, 10 a.m. Some place off Trafalgar Square. I looked it up.'

'You go,' Chamath told him. 'I have better things to do on a Sunday.'

'Yeah, like sleep.' Jonas crumbled his sandwich into pieces, popping them into his mouth. 'Oh well, suit yourself. If you don't need the money I guess you're one of the lucky ones.'

'But I do!' Chamath wanted to shout. 'My father wants me out of the house by the end of the month, I really don't know what to do; I'm broke as it is.' But he remained silent. He was too shy to expose so much of his soul to another man: unlike women, they were not built to take the weight of other people's sorrows.

After work, armed with two bottles of rosé he rang Jamila's bell.

'I need your help, please, I should have spoken to you before about this,' he said all in a rush.

She looked at the bottles in his hand. 'What's this? A bribe?' She paused a moment, as if considering. 'You'd better come in, then.'

The TV was on low. He noticed she didn't bother to turn it off or even mute it. She had covered her head today in a strip of bronze cloth. He couldn't help admiring her strong, slightly backward-sloping features, the temple goddess of some immigrant cult superbly indifferent to the small-time miseries of her followers. If she knew the secrets of life she was not about to let you in on them. All you could do was sit at the top of the temple steps and hope.

'My father wants me out of the flat by the end of the month. We need to get a tenant to pay the mortgage.'

She looked at him. 'Well you can't move in with me, if that's what you're after,' she said sternly.

He grinned. 'Not such a bad idea, is it? Now that you come to mention it.'

'Let's get this clear,' she said ignoring his flippancy. 'You want to let your flat. Your flat.' Her mouth twitched.

'Why? What's wrong?'

'Have you taken a good look at it lately? When was the last time you ran a hoover over it?'

He didn't like to admit he had never possessed a hoover. 'Will you help me get some agents to have a look? Use your charm to persuade them to take it on?'

'Carpets,' she said. 'Curtains. And get that hideous yellow turmeric stain off the work surface in the kitchen. A good industrial cleaning job, that's what you want.'

His heart sank. It wasn't the cleaning that worried him. It was the soft furnishings.

She looked at him shrewdly. 'You like it bare, don't you? You're one hell of a weird guy, you know that? Listen to me, people want a place to look like home—however desperate they may be to have a roof over their heads. And there's a lot on the market, I know that, so you're going to have to work really hard.'

He looked around her flat and envied her. The

council paid her benefits, she was in the system, she knew her rights. The book of council rules was her bible, as it was to every legal immigrant.

'And what you need most of all is money. What're your finances like?'

He looked sheepishly at the bottles of wine. 'Nothing more till pay day.'

'But you must have something saved up, big boy like you?'

He said nothing.

She sighed in exasperation. 'Oh Chamath, you're impossible. You're not cut out for life here, you know that? Go back to your own country where there are people to pick up the pieces. Here there's no one, can't you understand that?'

'Well, there's you,' he said softly, nuzzling her.

She shook him off. 'You wish.'

She got up from the sofa to signify that the consultation was over. He stood up too, reluctant to leave this haven of security. 'But if you ever need a sofa to kip down for the night, there's this.'

'Thanks,' he said hugging her hard, drawing comfort from the strength of the embrace.

'The sofa, mind. Nobody said anything about the bed.'

But upstairs on the floor he stretched his spare lean frame luxuriously against the carpetless floorboards, allowing his mind to roam over the topography of the flat. *So it needs to look more like home, does it?* he thought, working himself up. *Isn't this home enough?* Do they want to wrap me up in softness and bury me in strips of cloth and carpet? This is the corrupt foreign language they have all learnt by living here, he thought in rage, the essential middle-class vocabulary of city life. Is this the price I too have to pay for staying on?

Chamath jumped off the moving Number Eleven bus and ran down the Strand, cutting through side streets into St Martin's Lane. Past Freed's, past the Coliseum. He ran past Falconbury Court first time without realizing, and had to double back. He looked in vain for a name board at the entrance which might say *Embassy Services* but there was nothing. The green-glossed door swung open when he pushed it to reveal a narrow ancient staircase. He took the steps two at a time, up the wooden winders that creaked under his flying weight.

Jonas didn't look at all surprised to see him. 'I knew you'd come to your senses,' he said cynically. 'You're late. Last bloke just went in.' There were three guys sitting there with Jonas, all in their twenties, all with that breathlessly expectant, hopeful expression on their faces that he recognized so well. It was like looking in a mirror.

'What did they ask you?' he whispered.

'Ask?' There was a bemused look in Jonas's eyes. At that moment the last candidate came out of the inner room. He glowered at each of them in turn and exited, crashing down the stairs in protest. The sandy-haired man Gary who had come out with him saw Chamath and smiled.

'Ah, the sleeping beauty. We thought you weren't coming; that you'd lost your nerve at the last minute. Come in, come in, don't be afraid.' He flicked his fingers in the direction of the closed door and Chamath followed him in.

The inner room had the vaguely clubby look of a Georgian townhouse interior. A frayed Turkey carpet, a leather-topped table and panelled walls. The ceilings were low and the timber floor sloped. In a corner, rather incongruously, stood an old-fashioned grey filing cabinet. Leaning against it was the tall man, Mike. Chamath noticed that Gary had a clipboard in his hands.

'Right, get your kit off then.'

'*What*?'

'Your kit. Off. All of it.'

It was the strangest job interview Chamath had ever been to. He stood naked under the chandelier while they walked round him. He felt like a prize bull at an agricultural show. The balding carpet felt scratchy under his feet.

'Bit thin, aren't you?'

'Write down "*swimmer's physique*",' Mike told Gary.

They came to the front and paused a moment.

'I didn't know Asians came in that size.'

Gary giggled. 'An Asian XL? Contradiction in terms, surely?' Producing a camera from somewhere, they took his picture.

Mike looked at him curiously. 'Where did you get your accent from?'

'Oh, here and there,' Chamath said cagily.

'You sound like Norton Knatchbull. Gary, doesn't he sound exactly like Norton Knatchbull?'

Do I give a toss who Norton Knatchbull is? Just let me put my clothes back on! Chamath thought in sudden rage as he shivered. Any minute now this XL will turn into an XS.

'Right, get dressed and wait outside with the others. Oh, we need a name for you. Doesn't have to be your real one, you know.'

'I know,' said Gary. 'Let's call him Norton. *Norton*. How about that?'

Chamath went back out. He recognized the expression on the other faces now. Not breathless hopeful expectation at all, but sheer relief—that nothing more had been asked of them. Jonas was looking at him with a sly, slightly malicious look on his face.

'You were expecting something like this. You *knew*,' Chamath said angrily.

There was a flash in Jonas's eyes. 'Know? How would I know?' He looked round the room, then dramatically tapped his chest. 'Did *I* ask you to come? Am *I* asking you to stay?'

Chamath remained silent, glued unhappily to his seat.

'The thing about Embassy Services,' said their future employer, 'is that we're *not* your employer. We're your friend, your guide. You're in this purely for yourselves, remember that.'

'In other words, don't call us when you're in trouble,' Jonas murmured next to him. He called out loudly, 'So what are we, then? Fancy boys? Male escorts?'

Mike flinched. 'Please. We don't use those words around here. You are what we in the trade call *professionals. Professional companions.* You are paid to make people happy. If you're good at the job you stand to make an absolute fortune.'

'And the rates?' asked Jonas relentlessly.

'Thirty pounds for a four-hour session. This could be from 6 p.m. to 10 p.m. if you're required for a concert or play; 7 to 11 at night if it's dinner. Occasionally 10 till 2 in the morning for a dance. Who here has a suit?'

Chamath put up his hand.

'I have a white suit,' said Jonas. 'Will that do?'

'It most certainly won't. The punter doesn't want to draw attention to you. *Good-looking* and *discreet*, those are your watchwords. I suggest as soon as you get a little money, invest in a dark suit. Doesn't have to be new. You can get one in a second-hand shop. Now, does anyone have a dinner jacket?'

Again Chamath raised his hand, thinking of the fifteen-pound dinner jacket he had picked up at an Oxfam shop during his Oxford days.

Mike looked at him. 'I can see you're going to be a star,' he said.

'What happens,' asked Jonas, 'if they want us to stay the night?' There were uneasy sniggers all round.

'Entirely up to you,' said Mike. 'It's an additional fifty quid, but that's between you and God and the client. We don't get involved in that. In fact, we don't even want to know.' He shuddered slightly.

'So what's your cut? What do *you* get out of it?'

'Us? We're the facilitators, if you like. We get an introductory fee up-front from the client.'

'All we ask,' said Gary cutting in, 'is for you to call the numbers on your card every morning at 11 sharp. If there's a client, we give you their name and address over the phone. Your job is to turn up on time, all neat and scrubbed up. Is that clear? You don't have to see us again, you don't have to come here. Anybody asks, you never met us in your life. Understood? Right, any questions?'

One of the other guys put up his hand. 'If we don't call?'

'Somebody else gets the job. If you don't call three

days running you're off our list. Get that? No amount of whingeing will get you back on.'

'Rather like baseball,' said Gary giggling. 'Three strikes and you're out. No appeals.'

'Just one more question,' Jonas said slowly. 'What are these people actually like?'

Mike looked thoughtful. 'You'd be surprised really. Ordinary people. Not glamorous like in films. Some of them have saved up months for this treat. Girls in offices, old-age pensioners, men on business.'

'*Men?*' Chamath burst out before he could stop himself. 'I don't—can't do men!'

Mike looked at him dangerously, the look of a monk turned rabid. 'Do you want to fuck off now before you waste any more of my time?'

But he must have known Chamath wouldn't get up and go, because he continued as if there had been no interruption, 'Just one more thing. Please collect your money up-front. I can't stress this enough. Once a punter gets to know you, becomes a little friendly, that's when it gets dangerous. That's when they feel they can take liberties—it's all a bit of a lark, you're not really in it for the money. You're their friend after all, *you* won't mind. So be clear. If there's no talk of payment in the first five minutes, ask for it. If it's not forthcoming, leave. Is that understood?

'Oh, and very important. You are not to give your number or address to the client. All transactions through us. If you're good there'll be call-backs, but the client will have to go through us. This is for your safety.'

'Yeah, right,' murmured Jonas.

They all trooped down the stairs and out into the sunshine like a group of undergraduates after a tutorial, and Jonas and he split from the others.

'There now, wasn't too bad was it?' Jonas said as they walked along the Strand, looking into shop windows.

He said nothing.

'What, still sorry you came?'

Chamath could see there was a glow to his good-looking, insolent features almost as if they were lit from within. He thought: How lucky they were, people like that! Their way ahead was sure-footed and clear, they seized that ribbon of life with confidence, twisting it this way and that to suit their every whim and fancy, even knotting it sometimes out of sheer wilful bloody-mindedness. How different from him whose every step was blind with indecision, weighted with the agonies of a lifetime.

'You realize we're free at last of the Home Office? There's nothing to connect those two wankers to us. Only some fake names in a file and some photos. Nothing from us because we didn't sign anything. No contract.'

But all Chamath could hear was the recording in his head which kept going: *Don't do men, can't do men.* And the other which answered, *So you don't have to.*

Just don't call. Three strikes and you're out.

'Oh, lighten up!' Jonas said, clapping him on the back. 'You're Sri Lankan, remember? You're trained to take this kind of shit without complaining. It's what you're good at. It's the national characteristic.'

'Thanks,' said Chamath. 'I deeply appreciate that.'

'Where were you?' Jamila asked when he got back home. She was standing in the entrance hall in a headscarf, with bucket and mop, detergents and a shiny red hoover. Chamath thought with a grin: all she needs now is the endless granite floor of Heathrow Airport to mop, with plump jets popping up and down behind the plate glass windows. But he held his tongue because he could see she was in no mood for levity. In fact she was extremely annoyed.

'What are *you* smiling at?'

'Nothing,' he said, his mouth puckering up. 'You look yummy like that.' He leant over. 'How about a little something before we get started?'

'*Chamath, let go!* I wasted most of my morning on your account. If you want to do this on your own I'm going back in.'

'No, no, I'll be serious. *Promise!*' He manhandled her up the stairs.

Tuesday morning Jamila had organized for the estate

agent to come round and give her considered opinion on Chamath's flat. There was a mammoth cleaning job to be done. Together Jamila and he scrubbed the bathroom and wiped down the kitchen counter-tops (the turmeric stain refused to budge). There was no point hoovering the bare floorboards, the dust was too plentiful. In the end Chamath mopped them with soapy water. Watching her balance precariously on the window sill trying to wash the outsides of his sash windows he was touched with tenderness for her, her willingness to sacrifice so much time and effort for what was essentially a stranger's problem. There was a loyalty there that he had become unused to, living in the big city.

As the afternoon progressed he could see she was actually enjoying herself. 'We'll get there, Chamath,' she said softly. 'We'll get this sorted.'

There was a niggling worry in her use of that word *we*.

He almost said: 'You know it may not be necessary? You know there's another career option that just opened up?' But he didn't, because he knew only too well that hell hath no fury like a Good Samaritan scorned. Anyway it was the most shameful and dubious career imaginable; and he was beginning to love the idea of it. Why not? It would mean he didn't have to move out of the flat. There would be more than enough money to pay the mortgage. But even as he glowed with the anticipation of this future prospect he could feel the turbulence ahead, the rattle and shake of his moorings coming undone as he hurtled through the great white blankness of the London sky.

3

In the small front yard of the landladies' art deco villa was a dusty mango tree whose branches poked and peeped inquisitively into the old man's flat, situated above their now disused garage. How often the old ladies wished they could climb that tree! Of course they could have gone up the narrow vertiginous outside staircase that led to his room from the yard: and this they did quite often (like climbing Sigiriya, dear), but there was a limit to good neighbourliness. And the old man was quite skilled at repulsing all their kind offers of milk, sugar and dal.

'Can you believe it, dear, he says he gets *wind* from dal?'

'Well, *you* get wind from dal. Though you only seem to get it from my dal. I notice you manage quite well when it comes to the vadais from Greenlands.'

'Oh Bar, how could you! I *adore* your vadais.'

'Right, I'll make you some tonight, then, shall I?'

'Of course, dear. Though maybe not tonight, perhaps?'

The landladies particularly wanted to know what the old man was writing. If they went to the front garden they could see him at his window, click-clacking away at his typewriter. He appeared not to notice them. Oh if only they could have climbed that mango tree! But theirs had not been that sort of childhood—Daddy wouldn't hear of his little princesses climbing trees!—and sadly, sixty-odd was no age to start.

Inside the house were two bedrooms, one of which the ladies shared. The other was an all-purpose dumping ground for clothes, shoes, handbags and sundry items that had entered the house at some point and hadn't yet managed to effect an escape. There was, for instance, the Singer Sewing Machine circa 1910 operated by foot pedal. The ladies frequently talked about the ball gowns they would make on it. They gorged themselves on descriptions of the dresses, the colours, the materials, the details. So much so they were exhausted by the end of it, feeling, quite rightly, that they had already made these dresses. And they felt happy. Then there were Daddy's golf clubs from his days at the Royal Colombo Golf Club. After his death the ladies had briefly considered joining but the fees had proved prohibitive. Far more satisfying, then, to tramp the 18-hole golf course of their minds—followed, naturally, by cheese toast and gin and tonic on the clubhouse verandah at sundown, where the talk was all of birdies and eagles and other feathered friends of the golfing world—and all this in the comfort and convenience of your own home. Lastly, no inventory of the spare room was complete without the looming presence of Daddy himself, or rather his life-size portrait propped up against a wall in the corner, which the white ants had begun to eat. So far they had consumed the artist's signature, but Daddy himself remained uneaten.

The landladies were not used to housekeeping, indeed they had never done a stroke of work in their lives—because Daddy didn't like his little princesses et cetera, et cetera—but once a week Sakuntala the maid came in to run a cursory duster over things. For her part she realized that there was no way a single woman with just two hands could eradicate the golden dirt of ages, the patina of past lifetimes. In fact it was difficult not to be impressed by it all. Once on a lazy afternoon she had even tried identifying the age of the roll-top bath by the number of rings on it.

Sakuntala's employers weren't particularly bothered by her apparent lack of results. She was smart and presentable, she always had a lot to say for herself. Hers was a ceremonial role, and she had found this out quite early on: it enabled the ladies to drop the fact of her existence into their everyday telephone conversations with friends, peppering their dialogue with phrases like 'as the servant woman said to me' or 'Do you know what that stupid girl did yesterday at Wellawatte Market?'

It was a stroke of genius therefore when the landladies hit upon the idea of introducing Sakuntala into the relatively ordered calm of the old man's world upstairs.

'You take her up dear, I can't manage the stairs. My knees.'

'What do you mean *my knees*? Small people don't *have* knees.'

'Anyway, you're the one he fancies. You've made that very plain these last few days.'

'Fancies? I thought we had agreed he was a paedophile with homosexual tendencies?'

'Let her go by herself, then. She's a big girl.'

'That's what I'm afraid of. I know what men are like.'

'Oh, you *do*, do you?'

The mood was not very good downstairs that morning. But for the sake of a higher objective, a nobler goal, the unquenchable thirst for knowledge—What was being typed in that goddamned manuscript?—the sisters put their differences aside and pushed Sakuntala up the steep staircase. Alone.

The old man in all honesty was not much better at housekeeping than the downstairs lot; but the sparseness of his belongings, the frugality of his existence made his living that much easier. His typing for the day was just about to begin. From under his bed he pulled out a small tin trunk, enamelled in black with thin parallel gold lines around the edges. It had been his grandfather's old deed box. From this he carefully extracted the manuscript.

There was a knock on the door. Before he could answer, it was flung open. On the threshold stood a pretty girl in plaits.

'Me Sakuntala. Madams want me clean room 500 rupees a day one day week,' she said, all in one breath.

Five hundred rupees a day, one day a week, meant 2,000 a month, an amount that went against the grain of the old man's self-imposed monasticism. But he knew that it was politic to keep his landladies happy. After all, it wasn't only about the money was it? There had been emotions invested in this place all those years ago whose resonance he could still hear, ringing softly in the stones of its construction. In truth, wasn't that why he was here? With a game plan to his actions so long term and tenuous he could hardly voice it for fear it wouldn't come off?

Anyway, he couldn't help noticing what a fine pair of legs Sakuntala had on her.

'What that typing?' she asked. Her English was as atrocious as the old man's Sinhala, but they were able to meet happily in the middle ground of that war-zone, in that no man's land where dismembered limbs of Sinhala and English lay scattered and bleeding, ready for scavengers like him to pick up.

Lightning quick, Sakuntala leant over and had a peek at the manuscript. 'You know I have A level English? Only thing, can't read, no?' She giggled. 'My teacher worse. He no read, no *speak*, even.'

The old man reluctantly locked up the manuscript in the tin trunk and pushed it back under the bed, to Sakuntala's chagrin.

'You clean, I leave,' he said. 'After, I come back.' He placed a 500-rupee note on the table before he left. The landladies watched this new development with great interest from the downstairs window as the old man replaced the latch on the garden gate and disappeared up Galle Road.

'We have half an hour, I reckon,' said Ginnie. 'Are you ready for the ascent? Are your knees up to it?'

'Knees? What knees? Small people don't *have* knees. I thought you knew that,' replied Bar. 'Come on, what're you waiting for? *Beam me up, Scottie!*'

It rained all through Monday. The sort of rain England does so well, soft and unyielding, the fine spray of drops defying gravity, going up Chamath's nose as he ran for the bus. Inside Val's cabin it smelt of dog, which was strange really because there were no dogs for miles around. He and Jonas were issued with wellies because the site was one huge pool of mud. They were put to man one of the mixers. They worked in tandem like a pair of ballroom dancers—one retreating the other advancing—shovelling in gravel and sand alternately. Three of gravel to two of sand to one of cement. Once the stuff was in they waited briefly till it was mixed, then tapped it out the other side before starting again.

At five minutes to eleven Jonas said: 'Come on then. You coming or what?'

Chamath followed him to the single phone box across the road by the playground. They squeezed in out of the rain, wedging the door open because of the smell of piss inside. There were cards pasted to the inside of the phone box of jolly, buxom ladies willing to cane your seat for a small price. The first number was engaged. Jonas tried the other number on the card and got through.

'Yes, it's me, Jonas Williams . . . yesterday . . .' Outside the rain had got worse and Chamath huddled in. 'Nothing? All right then, I'll call tomorrow, shall I? . . . What, next week? Yeah, sure, I'll be available. Ta, mate, bye!' He put the receiver down looking disappointed. 'Too soon, they say. We only registered yesterday. But there may be a photo shoot next week.'

Chamath got through first go. 'It's me Chamath,' he said, 'I mean Norton.'

'Oh, *Norton*!' said Mike. 'Mr Posh. Well have I got good news for you! Tasty job. Concert at the South Bank, Queen Elizabeth Hall. Thursday evening. Punter wants you to meet him six sharp at the box office. Do you have a stripey tie?'

'I think so.'

'And white shirt. Customer wants you in white shirt and stripey tie.'

'I'll look like a schoolboy.'

There was a chuckle at the other end of the line. 'Maybe that's the idea.'

'I can do schoolboy,' Chamath said with a grin. 'If the money's right.' He stopped, shocked at himself. I can't believe I just said that, he thought. He felt light-headed and weak, like a man whose lottery ticket has just come up.

Jonas put his arm round him as they walked back to the site. 'I'm proud of you, fucker. We'll make a whore out of you yet.'

'Tell me something,' Chamath said. 'Doesn't it worry you at all, getting into something like this?'

Jonas looked at him, mildly annoyed. 'There's wankers like you who can afford to have a conscience. Then there's the rest of us with bills to pay, people to look after. This is the big city. You do what you do to get by.'

It occurred to Chamath that there was more than a hint of defensiveness in his voice. He had given it more thought than he cared to let on. 'It's not that I have a conscience,' he replied. 'Just curious, that's all.' But three more hours at the cement mixer in the powdery drizzle and Chamath found that his confidence had somewhat evaporated. They walked home up Ladbroke Grove, stopping at the caff on the corner to buy a burger and fries, soggy with grease. 'Aren't you getting anything?' he asked Jonas.

'No, mate. There's stuff at home,' Jonas said vaguely. They parted company at the Harrow Road junction. Though they were buddies neither had ever been in the other's house: it wasn't that sort of friendship.

By the time he got home and went upstairs, there were yellow slashes of late sunlight coming through the grey of the sky. He stripped off his sodden clothes and towelled himself dry. The heating wasn't working properly—his father had been conned into a system of convector heaters by a glib salesman (anything for a bargain, in the true Sri Lankan style) and they had been totally inadequate from day one. He looked sorrowfully at his clothes which lay in a steaming heap in the middle of the floor. Nothing would be dry enough to wear tomorrow. He had three T-shirts which he wore in strict rotation, and a single pair of jeans. I could wear my fifteen-quid DJ to work and stun them all, he thought wryly. Then he began to think of his new career. He opened the cupboard and took the dinner jacket out. There was a slight tear under the armpit but it wasn't visible when you wore it. He put it on. It fitted tightly—too tightly—across the chest. I must stop doing bench press, he thought. I can't afford to buy another one, and who knows when I'll need this for work?

Wearing just the dinner jacket he wandered round the unlit flat, moodily eating his burger and chips while the sky darkened again to an angry black. There was no sound from below. He put on his shorts and went downstairs. He had barely knocked when she opened the door.

'All set for tomorrow?' she asked brightly.

'Set for what?'

You could see the look of exasperation on her face. 'Oh, Chamath, don't tell me you've forgotten already?'

'Forgotten? Course not,' he bluffed. 'I was only teasing!' He had no idea what she was talking about. Then he remembered. The estate agent was coming round first thing in the morning. He was meant to have got permission to be late in for work. He was going to be in trouble now. Val's a good bloke, he thought. He'll understand. I can't help it if my life's got complicated all of a sudden.

He enveloped her in a bear hug.

'Chamath get off, you stink!' She pushed him away. 'Go and have a bath.'

He grinned. 'Yeah, but it's a good stink, isn't it?'

He liked having a bath in her bathroom. Her hot water system was that much better. 'Will you come and soap my back?' he called out.

She sat on the edge of the bath and soaped him,

making little noises of exasperation. But he could see that beneath her annoyance she was secretly pleased. Turning his head away from her he smiled.

Together on the sofa they watched TV, all those mindless quiz shows and soaps she loved, that were part of the ordered system of her life. At one point she turned to him and said, 'What?'

He shook his head. 'Nothing.'

When it got late she led him to bed, where he buried himself in her, immersed in those notes so deep the ear cannot hear nor the nose smell, and of which the heart has only the vaguest possible understanding.

The landladies were having a gala time. They poked and pried in every corner, through all the old man's belongings. It was turning out to be a fully comprehensive snoop. First of all they tried picking the lock of the tin trunk with a hairpin.

'It's a good thing I had hairpins on me.'

'Yes, dear. We all know your hair is thick and long, and mine short and stringy. You don't have to rub it in.'

The hairpin got stuck in the lock. Finally Sakuntala managed to pull it out with a pair of pliers the old man had kept to operate the stove which was missing its knobs. Ginnie had come across a very old, very grey pair of boxer shorts that she put on her head (to get us into a party mood, dear), and indeed there was a distinctly festive air to the little party upstairs.

Ginnie struck poses. With her strong angular features she thought she looked particularly like Katherine Hepburn as Eleanor of Aquitaine in *The Lion in Winter*. Bar thought she looked more like Mother Immaculata from Our Lady of Victories Convent, Moratuwa. Though not as dark, of course.

There were two photos pasted rather haphazardly on the wall. One was of a tanned man with a very fair girl, her frizzy blonde hair tied back. She had a nose almost in line with her forehead, and angular features. Behind them was a curved bay and the sea. It looked like Unawatuna, though it was too fuzzy to tell.

'Why, Ginnie, she looks exactly like that tourist who stayed here once. You remember? The one who was sleeping with the tour guide?'

'Sleeping? I don't remember anyone sleeping with anyone else. I think I would have remembered if any *sleeping* went on.' Ginnie paused. 'Actually I think she looks like me. Younger of course.'

'You? But she's white.'

'Well, I was white once. Daddy used to call me his little white princess, if you remember. That's why he left me the house.'

'Now don't get started on that. You know how it upsets me.'

They turned their attention to the other picture. It

was of the old man in his young days. He had his arm round a black girl with wiry red hair that sprang out round her in a dramatic halo. They both looked solemn, almost resentful, as if the cameraman had taken the picture without their permission.

'She's not very pretty, is she.'

'Now, Ginnie, don't be unkind. Just because she's darker than you.'

'But look at him. What amazing looks! A face that could stop traffic.'

'You mean like a traffic warden's?'

'They must have been a couple, mustn't they?'

'Why? I thought we had agreed he was a misogynist with bipolar tendencies.'

'And a tax inspector.'

'I don't know, but he looks mighty familiar to me.'

'Oh, you say that about everybody.'

In the midst of this, Sakuntala floated around with her Gehantex duster, artfully flicking here and there. Appearance was all. So it was she who spotted the old man standing at the doorway, wheezing slightly after the climb.

'Mmm, mm,' she said gesticulating wildly, her atrocious English deserting her at this vital moment.

'Why, Sakuntala, whatever is the matter?'

They turned and saw the old man.

'I'll thank you,' he said, his voice low and dangerous, 'not to mess with my belongings.'

The old ladies clattered out of the flat, with little whinnies and squeals of apology. It was only when she was halfway down the staircase that Ginnie realized she was still wearing the old man's shorts on her head, flapping wildly. In one magnificent move worthy of Eleanor of Aquitaine herself she swept them off her head and hurled them up the stairs, where they landed with an apologetic sigh on the top step.

When he opened his eyes she was still asleep. Her magnificent chocolate-coloured breasts were splayed apart, the cleft between them wide and shallow and dished, space enough to drive his head through, burning her skin with his day-old stubble.

She opened her eyes. 'Don't look at them,' she warned sleepily and turned over. Gently he turned her back.

She smiled. 'I always wanted WASP breasts,' she said dreamily. 'Those little pointy things you don't need a bra for.'

'I like these,' he whispered.

'Well don't like them too much. Go upstairs and tidy up. The agent will be here before you know it.'

His clothes were still in the heap he had left them the night before. The flat looked relatively neat and tidy, thankfully, because he had hardly been there to mess it up. He wriggled into his jeans, limp and soggy, though partly stiff in places that had dried out. They creaked as he walked, exuding a faint aroma of wet dog. It was like wearing cardboard as he limped around, his skin recoiling in revulsion at every step.

The doorbell rang at 9.30 sharp.

'Constance,' said the agent, extending a beautifully manicured hand. She swept past him with a smile towards someone else. Turning round, he couldn't believe his eyes: Jamila in a rust-coloured suit, bumfreezer jacket and short skirt, standing against the open doorway of her flat, her hair backlit in a glowing red halo. The two girls greeted each other like long lost friends, going up the stairs, hardly giving him a second glance.

Chamath marvelled at how confident and self-possessed they were, like children playing at being grown-ups, children who had mastered the sophisticated and tricky language of the city. But with Jamila he knew the truth beneath the image—the pliable innocence of her brown body, laid out on a bed of blue roses and yellow zigazags—and he was not fooled.

The girls stood in the middle of his sitting room in silence.

'See what I mean?' said Jamila.

Constance looked at her and giggled. Neither looked at Chamath who stood behind them, an uneasy bystander. Constance looked down at the damp patch left behind by his clothes and looked up at the ceiling. 'Is there a leak?' she asked. Without waiting for an answer the two girls clip-clopped across the bare floorboards to the bedroom, Chamath limping behind them in his damp jeans.

'Where's the bed?' she asked even though she could plainly see there wasn't one. And suddenly Chamath saw it all through her Sloaney, pearls-and-twinset eyes for what it actually was: a curious émigré existence devoid of pleasure and satisfaction, the cell of a monk of some obscure and esoteric sect right here in the heart of NW10. He wanted to put up his hands and say, *Please go away, I don't want to be shamed any more*, but he was too shy even to do that.

In the bathroom he noticed with disappointment that the white soap marks had reappeared on the midnight blue bathroom suite his father had been so proud of. He understood now that in Constance's world you were free to choose any colour you wanted for a bathroom as long as it was white. Onwards to the kitchen with its off-cut of blaring orange lino which Chamath had proudly bought for twenty pounds at the junk shop down the road. He could see its jagged zigzag edge for the first time—where the cut of his blunt Stanley knife had failed to follow the line of the skirting board.

He looked at the turmeric stain, its yellow insolence

bold against the all-white kitchen, and his heart was suddenly filled with love for it. It was the only thing on his side that morning. This is me and the world I represent, it seemed to say. I won't be going away in a hurry. If you're unhappy, I suggest it is you who should leave. All the words he lacked the courage to say out loud.

Constance went back to the sitting room and Chamath limped after her. She stood silently for what seemed a long time. 'When was this house converted to flats?' she finally asked.

'1979,' he replied. 'Six months ago.'

'I'll be brutally honest. This is one of the worst conversions I've ever seen. There's a lot on the market and you're going to have to work very hard to get anyone even to come and have a look at this place.'

'Tell us what he should do to get it up to scratch,' Jamila said. 'A checklist.'

Constance sighed. 'A good lick of paint. Carpets, curtains. Hanging space. *A bed.*' She looked meaningfully at Chamath. 'I tell you what. Why don't I come back in a month's time and check out progress? I wouldn't put it on the books just yet.'

He thought he could see her give a slight shiver of distaste but that might have been his imagination.

'By the way,' she said as she left. 'No dogs. I *know* you've had a dog in here. Prospective tenants do not like the smell of other people's dogs.' She smiled to show that there were no hard feelings. 'Oh, and I do hope your leg gets better.'

He was three hours late for work, and got the bollocking of his life from Val.

'You'd better watch your step, young fella-me-lad. You'll be out of here in no time if you do anything like this again. And by the way, when are you going to bring in your national insurance number?'

Fuck them all, Chamath thought as he silently filled the cement mixer. I'll show them. I'll soon have more money than I know what to do with, and then I won't need this poxy job anymore. I'd like to see his face when I hand in my resignation.

The old man sat at the desk looking out over Galle Road. He was chewing the end of a pencil. In front of him lay the typewriter unused, with a blank sheet of paper in it.

So this is what they think of me, he reflected bitterly. Some sort of circus freak to be made fun of behind my back. Leave now! he said to himself. You don't have to take this sort of crap from anyone. Almost inconsequentially, all the defects in the flat he had been prepared to overlook up to now—the leaky fridge, the hole in the roof through which water dripped on him when it rained at night—all these came to the fore. He thought back to that first interview with the landladies.

'What exactly did you do in the UK?' Bar had asked.

'Oh, this and that,' the old man replied reluctantly. 'I was a builder once.'

'Very good, then you can fix any little thing that needs to be fixed. Not that there's much,' she assured him briskly. 'It's in mint condition.'

'Mint,' agreed Ginnie.

The old man forebore to mention that builders were the laziest people imaginable. It was almost a given that they lived in the most neglected, dilapidated homes. It was like hairdressers going around with the worst hair-cuts. Instead he said with a smile: 'It looks very nice to me.'

Ginnie smiled back. He looked at her angular features, her nose in an almost unbroken line with her forehead, her frizzy hair. *Remember me,* he willed her silently, *remember me. Cast your mind back.*

Plainly, she couldn't. All she saw was a returnee, a slightly absurd figure of fun, living the life of a hermit in a broken-down Bamabalapitiya flat.

It is amazing, he thought, the disparity that exists between what others actually think of us, and what we fondly imagine they think. It allows us to preen and strut with all the misplaced bravado and foolish confidence of an idiot. But then he thought, if he was an idiot so was everybody else, with their own delusions of self-worth. And when he realized this he felt suddenly happy. 'You'll take the shape of any cup you're poured into,' Jonas had said. The water had silently, unaccountably, crept in from nowhere to fill his container to the brim, to assume with quiet ease and satisfaction the shape of his current existence.

4

Because it's the first time you've ever done this you scrub up extra well, showering and shaving, making sure your clothes are spotless. It's only when you're more seasoned that you realize the punter actually likes you a little rough, it pleases them because there's this question of ownership here: nobody can truly be convinced they own you unless you're a little incomplete, so they can walk all over you with their patronization, and their bright ideas for your improvement. And maybe they get their sexual kick out of a bit of rough anyway, who knows?

You can smell the joe long before you see him, wafting up to you in clouds of cheap scent, as if he's rolled over and over in air-freshener. Except you know somehow it's probably the most expensive thing going, distilled from the hand-harvested sweat glands of the now-extinct Arctic lemur or something like that. It all smells the same to you, but please don't tell him that; it'll probably give him a nervous breakdown or something. So you flash your hundred-watt smile and stand politely to attention.

'Norton!' he says in a voice both fruity and unctuous, the sort of voice a wedding cake would have if it could speak. 'Norton, Norton, *Norton*! Come, let me take a good look at you!' He examines you minutely, his head bowed, his plump hands placed on a little dome of a stomach. And while he's examining you, you examine him: his white forehead, high as a marble mausoleum, his Roman nose, his curious blue-black hair cropped close to his curiously unlined face. And when he beams, you silently breathe a sigh of relief that your student credentials haven't let you down. And then you realize with horror that your stripey school tie is twisted and he can see the name-tape (Cash's, of course!) sewn to the underside proclaiming your real name, and you hurriedly tuck it back into your shirt. But he's too busy propelling you through the foyer to notice, bestowing regal glances right and left, an emperor with his new birthday toy

And you're sitting now in the front row of the dress circle and he's especially pleased when you open your mouth and the Oxford accent tumbles out (*I didn't pay for that, is it extra?*) and he's smiling with everyone, especially the musicians. Turns out he knows the first violinist and also the bassoonist, and you get the idea you're only here so he can score points over them. And they're playing Tchaikovsky's *Capriccio Italien* and *Marche Slave*, the sort of music your classics master at school always considered kitsch, but which you find you're quite enjoying after all.

And when the music's over the joe takes you under the arches at Waterloo Bridge to an Italian restaurant called Il Pappagallo and he's mightily pleased when he finds he has to teach you the proper way to eat mussels (till then the only muscles you knew were the ones on your arms) and afterwards when he invites you back to his flat for a nightcap, ha ha, you invent a sick mother waiting up for you.

'Mother? Ah, what would we do without them!' he says. 'I have one too, living in the flat with me. Luckily, mine's a little deaf,' he adds with a lascivious wink.

'Well, that's funny, because mine's a little dead,' you want to reply but you don't because that's *one sick Mother* of a joke, and not likely to go down well in present company. So you just stand there looking at him, while the icy wind in this concrete Waterloo jungle rips through your thin shirt. He stands there too, hoping his luck will turn, and it's getting a little embarrassing. You're feeling sorry now. He seems a genuinely good bloke and it wouldn't kill you to spend the evening with him, bonding over live-in mothers; but you know somehow the bondage he has in mind is of a very different sort.

So he pulls out an additional tenner and puts you

into a taxi home ('Because we can't have your mother worrying, can we?') and you stop the taxi as soon as it turns the corner, and you pay the driver a pound so you have nine left and you walk home. All the way.

And it's the easiest thirty-nine pounds you ever made in your life, and you think: Why didn't anyone tell me about this before?

The Victorian terraced houses of Hiley Road were narrow and tall and almost identical to each other, stacked together like playing cards standing on end. In 1979, converting one of them into flats was a new idea.

'You just put a wall down the middle here,' said the Pakistani developer who showed them round, 'and hey presto, you have two flats.'

Chamath's father had been amazed and delighted. He had bought the flat for all the wrong reasons. It was a new idea, and he was nothing if not a sucker for new ideas. He bought it to help a fellow Asian out of his financial difficulties.

'I'll give you a 20 per cent discount if you exchange within the fortnight,' the developer offered generously. 'Between exchange and completion there'll be plenty of time for me to paint the place up, put in the heating and the carpets. Of course I would need to use your deposit to do this.'

As it happened there was not only a generous discount on the sale price; there was an even more generous discount on their expectations. When the time came to complete, nothing further had been done.

'I warned you not to let him use the deposit,' said the lawyer. 'I *told* you how irregular it was. I warned you of the dangers.'

'So what do we do now?'

The lawyer shrugged. 'Sue him for return of deposit. Find something else to buy. Of course it'll cost you a packet in legal fees.'

That did it. Chamath's father was one of those rare people who was all for taking risks as long as they were esoteric enough. (Buying a flat in London had been one glorious gamble as far as he was concerned.) But to sue somebody in courts for return of the money you were owed was too prosaic an idea for him to entertain. When called upon to champion worthwhile but dull causes he was apt to become curiously tight-fisted.

'Never forget that your ancestor was Lord High Treasurer to the last King of Kandy,' he said to Chamath. (He said this at least once a week.) 'We get our financial acumen from him. From him we have inherited the *money gene*.' Chamath often wondered whether the fall of the Kandyan kingdom had been due not to the British at all, but to the plain damned foolishness of its last treasurer.

'Go ahead and complete the sale,' said Chamath's

father imperiously. The lawyer looked at him in amazement. 'Chamath here can put in the heating and the carpets. He can paint. He's an *experienced* builder, you know.' (Chamath looked at his father in amazement. At this time he had been working on the building site barely a fortnight.)

There were other reasons for his father's decision to go ahead. To pull out would have been to admit he had been cheated by a fellow Asian, that his judgment had been warped. But even more important, he had to attend the St Anthony's Ball in Colombo the following week, organized by the old boys. He had given his word he would be present and he was not about to break that. The sale went ahead.

All these thoughts kept swirling through Chamath's head like scenes in a film. In the foreground was Constance. *I'll be brutally honest with you*, she kept saying in her rah-rah accent. *Brutally, brutally honest, yah?* Meanwhile Chamath sat in the front row of the cinema hall, cowering in the dark.

'So?' said Jonas. 'Tell me.'

Chamath grinned and punched the air. 'Your turn next, mate.'

'They want me to do a shoot. Hard core.'

'I thought you had to be big to do stuff like that.'

'Fuck off. If you're going to be like that I won't give you the gory details.'

'That's a relief. Whatever you do, don't be an idiot, take precautions.'

'Try telling yourself that, mate.'

'What're you two yakking about, like a couple of old women?' roared Val. 'Get over here and unload this timber at once!'

When he got home that evening the door to Jamila's flat was wide open.

'Come in,' she called out. She was seated at the table with the Yellow Pages, under a reading lamp. The light reflected off the directory burnished her hair to a glowing bronze orb, a penumbra that moved as her head moved. 'I'm making a list of contractors. For your estimates.'

'Forget it,' he wanted to say. 'I'm not moving. I don't need to move.' But that would have meant explaining. Instead he sank down wearily on the sofa to watch her as she moved her index finger down the page, stooping over the book as she copied out names. He felt so cosy, so intimate just sitting there in her company. This could be a scene from my later life, he thought, when I'm married.

Married? He sat up. Who said anything about marriage? He felt embarrassed with himself, as if he had caught himself thinking obscene thoughts. He looked up and saw that she was observing him, and quickly looked away.

I don't love her, he thought. She certainly doesn't love me.

5

So you are on a train to Stratford, East London, and if you think Kensal Green is bad you should see this: a wasteland, with great gaps and gobs of space in between derelict buildings through which the wind whooshes triumphantly, and you shiver in your thin white shirt because this is not quite what you've been expecting. And when you get to the house it's not so bad, really, a double-fronted Victorian villa in what must have been once a posh street. And when she opens the door and says an over eager *Hello!* you realize she's much older than you had imagined in your prurient schoolboy mind. You have a lovely smile, she says, and you wish you could return the compliment. Her hair is dyed a traffic-reflector blonde. And as she flows down the passage in her girlie-girlie Monsoon dress, you notice to your right the sitting room painted dark grey, which has shelves with rows and rows of heads on them, hideous, nightmarish.

'Oceanic art,' she says airily. 'Probably the finest collection in the country still in private hands.' And she laughs, her girlie-girlie laugh.

And then you hear it, from the kitchen at the end of the passage, the sounds of a thousand whimpering creatures, the scrabbling of tiny feet, and you begin to think you are indeed in a nightmare.

'My little babies,' she says and for a moment you believe her, till you realize with a gush of relief they're only chihuahuas, twenty-four of them poking their black grape eyes at you from behind the dog gate; and you think, that's twenty-four too many for me. And then it hits you, the smell of them all over the house. Enough to make an estate agent proud.

'I thought we'd eat in here,' she says throwing open a door to the blood-red dining room. She pours you a glass of wine—red, of course—and sits you down in a straight-backed chair upholstered in Genoa velvet, and there is something both high camp and bizarre about this Grand Guignol theatre of a dining room. Any moment now you expect her to wheel in a live animal sacrifice, squirming and squealing underneath a bell-shaped silver dish-cover. Then again the live animal sacrifice she's got planned might well be you, who knows? You hear her saying something in the kitchen: she's talking to the dogs. It's just another day for her, a little red wine, a little intelligent conversation with the dogs behind the dog-gate. And though it's freaking you out, it is at the same time strangely normal. This could so easily be *your* life: another cosy domestic evening after a hard day at the office, dear; and you marvel yet again at how easy you find it, this fitting into other people's lives. And you would like to stamp on it, this ease, as if it were a worm, stamp on it really hard till its insides are splayed out all over the floor and on the soles of your shoes, because this is what you most despise about yourself, even though there is nothing you can do about it.

In between her numerous trips to the kitchen to bring in the plates of salami and olives she places an envelope by your plate.

'For the night,' she says and laughs, her girlie-girlie laugh.

Upstairs the bed has red satin sheets on it, and you're sure they haven't been washed for weeks because there's a certain waxiness to them. And there's a certain waxiness to her pale body too, years and years of potions and unguents applied with care to the thousand-year-old body that just popped out of its sarcophagus tonight specially for you, and you grin to yourself because really, it's just like making out with mummy.

And you're up pretty much the whole night because you can't sleep between sessions and you look at her mouth, slightly open with the exertion, the breath whistling in and out, and you notice the roots of her teeth exposed at the gums, and it hits you, the meaning of that expression *long in the tooth*.

And when it begins to get light you pick your clothes up off the floor checking to see whether the envelope with your eighty pounds is still there and you tiptoe out, down past the chihuahuas who begin to whimper expectantly because like you they haven't had a wink of sleep, and you pause a minute in front of the Oceanic heads, gleaming and malevolent in the grey half-light. Shall I take one? you think to yourself. Just one? *Please?* It'll solve all my problems, and she'll never know, and she certainly doesn't need it. But you don't. Because you're just a dumb-fuck at heart, aren't you, not really cut out for this sort of work at all.

And you walk back sadly through the bomb-damaged streets—and at this hour it really does look like Hitler's planes left only an hour ago—and you take the first train of the day home. And it is only then it strikes you: that perhaps, just *perhaps*, there are better ways to make a living.

Hiley Road was just coming alive. He watched the milk float deliver his pint, delaying his step so he wouldn't have to chat to the milkman. There was the same white light in the sky but for once he felt not exalted but strangely flat. Nursing a scalding hot mug of tea (PG tips, so much sugar you could stand the spoon up in it) he sat on the floor looking moodily up at the sky.

Was this what he wanted? It seemed to him he was at a point in his life where he could go in several directions. He could go the direction Jamila had taken, carving his own distinctive space, his own shadowy corner within the bright lights of the enormous solar system that was London. Or he could go back home, marry the girl his father might choose, and sink into immensely contented obscurity. In fact he was doing neither of these at the moment. He was spinning like some rogue planet totally out of control, only barely obeying the accepted norms and laws of gravity. He knew he was at the outer edges of the system now, travelling so fast it was almost too late to turn back. But not quite. So what did he want then?

The half mug of tea was cold. Chamath got up wearily. What he wanted actually was a long hot bath, to be scrubbed and pummelled, to be washed clean of the night he had just left behind. An hour later he was dressed and ready for work. The door downstairs opened a crack.

'Where were you last night?' she whispered angrily. 'I waited up for you!'

Through the gap in the door he could barely see her head but he could hear it, hissing in the dark, and for a moment he thought it was one of the Oceanic heads come back to haunt him.

'You don't have to whisper,' he said. 'There's no one else here.'

But she continued, mumbling in rage incoherently.

'I can't talk, I'm late for work,' he said shutting the door on her talking head.

On site there was an air of festivity. It was Friday, pay day.

Jonas regarded him curiously. 'You look knackered. Heavy night?'

Chamath made a face. 'And you? You never said how your shoot went.'

'What's there to tell?'

Chamath grinned. 'Got through a rubber or two?'

There was a pause. 'It was a gay mag. I'd rather not talk about it if you don't mind.'

They worked in silence for a while. 'You tell anyone here, I'll kill you. I mean that.'

Chamath felt a little stab of satisfaction. He thought to himself: it's one thing to rationalize these things in your mind; it's another to go out and actually do them.

Armed with his pay packet and last night's takings he went into an off-licence on the way back and bought a bottle of champagne. It felt quite like the old Oxford days. Back home he knocked on her door.

'What's this, a peace offering?' she asked looking at the bottle.

'I'm sorry I was in a rush this morning,' he said humbly.

'I go to all the trouble to make these lists. Why is

it that I'm doing all your worrying for you? Don't you understand the gravity of the situation?'

He opened the bottle and poured it foaming into two mugs. He gave one to her. 'Cheers,' he said lamely.

'And how do you think you're going to pay bills if you go around wasting money like this?' She took an angry gulp of champagne and sat down with a bump.

He looked at her and saw the regulated motion of her planet, spinning precisely in its orbit. Her life was just so, every penny accounted for, its route mapped among the stars for all eternity with a kind of parsimonious beauty, a meagre elegance. And to think I could have all this, he thought cynically. *What a treat!*

He made an effort to exit this fanciful mind of his, to pay conscious attention to her words, but the image of her kept blurring, as if there was something wrong with his eyes. At one point she wasn't in her robe at all but a sari, a Sri Lankan housewife heckling him for bringing home the wrong sort of fish from the market for the night's dinner.

'The thing is,' he said clearing his throat, 'I won't be needing to move out at all. I've got the money for the mortgage.'

It was her turn to stop, shocked. 'You mean I've been out of my mind with worry for nothing?' Her face creased with suspicion. 'What money?'

He hadn't intended to tell her but he had gone too far now to turn back. Reluctantly he began to talk about

Embassy Services, dragging the phrases out with care in measured and precise terms, laying them out for her inspection like an old-fashioned door-to-door salesman in Colombo.

With every word he could see her stiffen and flinch, every word a small and well-aimed blow. He forced himself to carry on, a sort of penance, till finally he came falteringly to a stop. There was silence.

She looked up, her face puffed and screwed up with what seemed like sheer physical pain. She took a deep breath. 'Let me get this straight. What you're telling me is, you fuck people for money?'

'It's only a job. It's not as if I have feelings for them or anything.' He gave an uneasy smile and reached out to touch her, but she moved back. 'Jamila, please,' he began, but she wasn't listening.

'You disgust me,' she whispered. She rose slowly to her feet, summoning all the strength she could muster. 'Get out,' she said hoarsely. 'I don't ever want to see you again, you little piece of shit. You *scum.*' She began to rant, but all he could see were the dark grey walls— the heads all talking at once, terrifyingly incoherent in a hundred different dialects, hissing and growling and whistling.

'And if you ever, *ever* see me in the corridor, don't even look at me!' she screamed. 'Understand?'

'What's it to her?' he thought puzzled as he closed the door. 'It's my life. It's my body.'

6

The land sloped gently down to the sea. In those days the Galle Road was no more than a sandy cart track that wound its leisurely way to the southern port of Galle, where the Portuguese invaders had first landed. The house occupied two and a quarter acres of land. It was single-storyed, with two wings that swooped round, partially enclosing a front court that afforded some protection from the merciless sea at the back. In modern estate agent's parlance you would have been hard pushed to describe it as anything more than a two-bed house; but this would not have taken into account the wing at the back, which contained the godowns, the stores, the kitchens, the servants' quarters; also the *kakusiya*, a Sinhala corruption of the Dutch *kakhuis* or shithouse.

Bar and Ginnie could remember the house from their younger days: the immense arch twelve foot wide by twelve foot high that separated the two halls, the kabook walls plastered with crushed coral, faintly blued; the floor of terracotta tiles one inch thick and one foot square, laid on the bias, and the creaking wooden Baroque windows (glass was out of the question in the seventeenth century when the house had been built).

'*Mon Repos*?' said Bar's and Ginnie's father when he inherited, for that was its name. 'How frightfully common. I think I'll call it *Bubbles*, instead.' If Bubbles was even more common, nobody had the guts to point this out to old Mr de Silva, the Ginger Beer King of Bambalapitiya. If you had made a personal fortune out of selling your own brand of ginger beer, why couldn't you own a house called Bubbles? In his white ducks and solar topee (lined in billiard-table green) and his silver-topped Malacca cane, he was a familiar figure in Bambalapitiya.

The de Silvas belonged to the Karawa caste, a community which had arrived in Sri Lanka from the Coromandel Coast of India, in successive waves of immigration throughout the second millennium after Christ. Of different race to the indigenous people, they had settled up and down the coast as boat-builders and fishermen. With the advent of the colonial invaders they had converted to Catholicism, the new religion giving them excellent moral license to make their fortunes on the sale of alcohol. (Buddhists of the time didn't drink. At least they said they didn't.) Mr de Silva's famous ancestor, Augustinho Rendrale, had at one time been proud possessor of almost every single arrack rent on the Colombo coast.

The fortunes of the Karawas rose and fell like the waves on which they rode their boats. In their day-to-day life they had a spirit of adventurism and devil-may-care bravado so woefully lacking in the indigenous farming communities of the central highlands, the Kandyans. After the boats and the alcohol came graphite. Sri Lanka was blessed with the purest graphite in the world, essential to the manufacture of guns. It is not too fanciful to say that the guns that went to war on both sides of both world wars of the twentieth century were forged in the mines of Sri Lanka. And the Karawas were at the forefront of this too. Not all were lucky, however, because not all had graphite on their land. *Dig here*, said old Mr de Silva. They dug, and struck rock. *Dig here and here*, he said. And they struck rock and more rock. It became something of an obsession with the old man, and long after the world wars were over he kept digging, for graphite that simply wasn't there. His estates were pitted and pockmarked with barren unproductive holes of shale, now filled with rainwater and dengue mosquitoes: and his fortunes likewise.

It was then that he turned his attention to ginger beer, this being the period Ginnie and Bar remembered best, a champagne existence that foamed and fizzed, fuelled by the bubbles of *de Silva's Nariya Ginger Beer*. NARIYA GINGER BEER PUTS THE LEAD BACK INTO YOUR

MAN'S PENCIL ran the slogan, and housewives ran out to buy bottles of the stuff to ginger up their lacklustre love lives. Arrack and ginger beer became the drink of choice for young married couples, and every evening the lady of the house could be seen on her verandah, holding a Nariya by the neck, waiting eagerly for her man to come home. Every day the old man tottered off to the bottling plant in Slave Island, wedged into a small plot of land between the Kompanna Veediya Railway Station and the Beira Lake. The cast iron girders and the corrugated iron roof of the plant rang to the sounds of his voice as he personally supervised the preparation of the ginger, the fermentation process and the bottling line. Any slackers on the line would get a sharp cut across their back from the Malacca cane.

If the old man was Ginger Beer King, then his daughters were the Ginger Beer Princesses; and this they never forgot, even after the bottling plant in Slave Island was sold to a multinational and the de Silva fortunes began to go flat again. (Bubbles had been knocked down and sold to pay Mr de Silva's debts and death duties, and the land sold, leaving the one small villa that had been built in the front garden for Ginnie.) But in those champagne days, many a young man had arrived at Bubbles to ask for the hand of one or other of the daughters. No man was good enough for Mr de Silva's princesses, and they were speedily ejected, often not before they had received a sharp cut across their backside from the de Silva cane. Though Gin and Bar were far too well bred to mention it now, this untold family history—this glittering backstory—occupied a greater part of their minds, informing their carriage and bearing when it came to dealing with lesser mortals. Like their present lodger.

'Is there any possibility, dear, that he might be in the least bit Karawa?'

'Not in the slightest. He's probably one of those dreadfully sly and slothful Kandyans.'

'But his hair, dear. Awfully curly, don't you think? *Kaffir* hair?'

'Oh, Bar, how could you!'

'No, I'm rarely wrong about these things. Explains why he's not the slightest bit interested in dancing to Victor Sylvester. But you just put some Kaffringha music on, he'll be down here before you can say *Robertson's Marmalade*.'

Sakuntala still went up once a week. But the sisters never followed after that first day's fiasco. In fact they had been very worried he would give notice; but promptly on the first day of the following month 18,500 rupees in a brown envelope had been posted under the grill door downstairs.

The landladies rejoiced and their confidence returned.

'I knew he couldn't possibly leave. He hasn't finished his tax report, for a start.'

'Where would he find another place like this?'

'Sometimes,' said Ginnie wistfully, 'I wish he'd be more detailed and exhaustive in his investigation. I wish he'd come downstairs and give us a thorough examination. I, for one, would be happy to show him everything I have.'

'Really, Ginnie, what a *dirty* thing to say.'

In a funny way, the payment had in fact put them back in the ascendant.

'After all, we were doing nothing wrong, were we? A landlord has every reasonable right to inspect his tenant's premises.'

'But not to wear his underwear on their head.'

'Oh, nonsense. That was just a bit of good clean fun.'

'Clean? *Clean?* Did you see the state of them?'

The old ladies decided they needed to celebrate, to seal their victory. So, after much deliberation they went out and bought themselves a puppy. A boxer named Shorts.

So you're sitting in this very small theatre, in the stalls, with the joe next to you. Only this time it's not a joe but a *josephine,* and you cannot believe how young she is, twenty-two, twenty-three—your age—and you think, surely she's young enough to find someone she doesn't have to pay? But you remind yourself you're not here to question the whys and wherefores of the situation so you take her hand, and her honey-coloured hair smells nice and the tip of her upturned nose is extremely kissable.

'Look,' she whispers dramatically, 'that's Princess Michael three rows up!' And it is indeed Princess Michael three rows up, and you actually don't give a damn but you get caught up in her excitement, 'And look at her pearls!' she whispers, and you notice the pearls—creamy and lustrous and so enormous just one of them would probably redeem the entire mortgage on your flat. And you put your arm round the back of your josephine's chair and she nestles her head on your shoulder and she feels so soft and sweet and fragrant you could have her for breakfast, lunch and dinner every day of the week; and you're so busy looking at her that the entire play goes by unnoticed.

Afterwards she takes you to Jo Allen's (a mistake, the music's too loud, you can't hear each other; you're getting to be quite the expert on these matters, aren't you?).

'I was living with someone for two years,' she says, making a moue of those edible lips. 'Then he left me.'

She has to shout over the fuzz of the music; and the loudness only serves to squeeze the pathos out of her meaning, leaving behind just the dried-out pulp of actual fact: the story of yet another pretty girl in the big city who has been left behind by a love-rat after he sucked out all he could. And your sympathy cannot compete with the music, so you squeeze her hand hard. What you would really like to do is lay her down and with your hands squeeze her all over, squeezing all that sympathy you have back into her: because only you know how much you have to give.

And when the meal is over and your time is up, you foolishly offer to accompany her back to her place in South Ken. It's a long walk but a fine night. You pass through the elegant calm of Hereford Square into the red-brick gloom of Rosary Gardens where she lives in a basement flat. She looks at you then, and you know she doesn't have the additional fifty to ask you in, and you could so easily say, I'll stay the night don't worry, it's a freebie, but you don't. Something happens. Some atavistic streak of cruelty kicks in and all of a sudden you realize who you are. You're the hard bastard for whom business is business and pleasure is pleasure; the shadowy man behind the *guichet* who's accepted the money and given the ticket. The transaction is complete: all that's left for you is to pull the metal grill down hard with a clank. Shut. To do anything else would be a betrayal of all the principles you stand for. (Principles, did you say? Ha!)

But when you get back home there's no sound from downstairs, and you wander round the rooms turning the lights on and off, on and off, one by one, and there's a hole in your heart the size of Sigiriya and you wonder: really, actually, honestly, who is it for?

The nights he wasn't working were the worst. It was not as if he had ever spent more than an evening or two every week with Jamila. But her presence below, the sounds of her moving—from sitting room to bedroom to kitchen like some furtive creature—had been the rock to which he had been anchored, the stable launching pad from which he had been able to fly untroubled in the white sky. She was still there: but any muffled noise that now came up only served to emphasize her absence. He couldn't get his head around this question of morality. How was it possible that what he found blameless she found despicable? Which was worse: to sell yourself to the highest bidder as he was doing (a transaction between two consenting adults) or, say, to scrounge council benefits (as he knew most legal immigrants did) thereby depriving more needy people of them? In her book his was by far the worse sin. Why? Only because that's what you were told: it came far higher up on the list, right up there with murder and coveting your neighbour's wife.

Don't look at me, don't even think of me, I am not here for you. It was unreasonable. He had done nothing wrong. At least, if he had done wrong to himself he had not done wrong to her. But in her eyes he had stopped being a human being. He was no more than a rat feasting on other people's garbage. He cursed himself for telling her, for being weak. He had only done so to seek in some perverse way her approval. Beware those who are foolish enough to want another man's sympathy and blessings, he thought. All you'll get is their scorn and derision and disgust.

The Kensal Rise Library was open late. He went round the corner to Bathurst Gardens, taking the book that had been lying by his sleeping bag unread these last two weeks. Other people's fiction seemed colourless and commonplace now, beside the lurid, strangely surreal facts of his own life.

The ordered calm of the library soothed him. The sandstone Ionic columns against the red brick walls, the Victorian cast-iron downpipes, all this spelt stability, immutability: they would be there long after he was gone; and by now he was almost all gone. There was a woman hunched up at a table, reading. She looked familiar, and he surreptitiously went round the side to take a look. But it wasn't her. Thank God, he thought with a gush of relief. I would not have had the courage to speak.

Jonas didn't turn up to work.

'Do you know where he is?' Val asked. He shook

his head. He didn't even know where he lived, to get a message through to him.

'Bloody better turn up soon,' Val said. 'His job is on the line.'

At 11 sharp Mike took his call. 'You have a job tonight in Wimbledon,' he was told. He took down the address and time. 'Some foreign woman. They may want more but that's up to you.'

'They?'

'I mean she. By the way, where's your friend? He didn't call yesterday. Tell him, one more day and he's out.'

'I'll get him to call you tomorrow, somehow,' Chamath promised. Though how he was going to do that he had no idea.

7

From Wimbledon Station you take Worple Road and you have no sodding idea, do you, how long this bloody road is? Just as you're about to give up you find Arterberry Road. When you ring the bell you think you've got the wrong house because two people answer the door, a man and a woman.

'No,' says the man smiling, 'you don't have to do me. Not unless you want to. She's the client. It's her treat. I ordered you for her.'

'What do you mean *my* treat?' she replies hotly. 'You know you're the one who'll get a kick out of this. It's for *you* we're doing this.'

You have to decide very quickly whether you want in or out on this one. It looks tricky and they want an all-nighter. But there's something about their fresh faces, their wholesome milk-and-honey innocence— and although they're older than you they're young, under thirty.

And you get along famously over two bottles of Rioja and what seems the sketchiest of dinners (a sort of creamed spinach soup with melted cheese on top).

'You know she's from Spain?' he says. 'She's descended from the Visigoths.' And you notice she has masses of frizzy blonde hair and green eyes, and a nose that disappears into her forehead in one continuous line.

'She lives in a castle,' he says. 'Can you imagine? With no electricity and no running water. And you know what? There are cows on the roof.'

'Of course there's electricity!' she replies spiritedly. 'There's a generator.'

'But nobody can afford the petrol to run it,' he says with a smirk.

'Stelios you bastard!' she says fondly, hitting him with a bread roll.

And when the second bottle is finished you really don't feel you're the professional and these are your joes. They're more like old school friends you ran into on the road, who invited you back to supper to talk of old times.

After the non-dinner they lead you to the bedroom, and he watches while you do her, and you find you don't really care he's watching because she has the sweetest breasts imaginable, round and so small you can almost put them whole into your mouth, and down there she's small too, and she grips you so tight she keeps you balancing on the edge, and every time you feel yourself falling over she somehow manages to bring you back upright, and you think: this is what saints must feel when they reach religious ecstasy. And finally when you do fall over, he bursts out laughing delightedly because to him it's an old old trick, one that after two years of marriage no longer surprises him. And you finally fall asleep in their enormous bed in this attic flat in Wimbledon, strangely comforted by their presence, his snores and her gently-rising-and-falling stomach, but as you go over the edge into sleep a niggling thought enters your mind: isn't two years too soon to be bored of each other that you need to start experimenting like this? But you shush yourself for being so disloyal, traitorous even, and then it occurs to you—and you really are too sleepy now to take this in—that you have already crossed that invisible border into their country, and you didn't even know.

In the morning you leap out of bed because you have overslept.

'What's the hurry?' they ask sleepily. 'Have some breakfast. We'll drop you home on the way to work.'

But you remember in time you're the hard bastard, and hard bastards don't give out personal details of their home life. Ever.

'It's OK,' you say, 'I'll take the tube.'

'We had fun, didn't we?' they ask.

Yes! yes! yes! you want to reply but you don't.

Then she writes down their number on a piece of paper. 'If you ever want to come over and hang out, please call,' she says. 'There's a home for you here.'

And your heart sort of melts into one slushy heap because nobody has ever done this to you, nobody has ever trusted you that much. And you realize they must have sensed something of the loneliness inside you, that dirty great hole the size of Sigiriya. And you leave quickly, before they can see the tears welling up in your eyes.

He sprinted down the length of Worple Road. Two buses overtook him, but by the time he reached the next stop they were long gone. At Wimbledon tube station he hurled himself on to the District Line. At Earls Court there were interminable delays, and by the time he reached Hippodrome Mews he was two hours late.

Val's face was like thunder but he didn't say anything. Jonas had turned up to work. He had a black eye which was beginning to go purple, an ugly stain spreading across that side of his face. Chamath knew better than to ask what had happened or even laugh, which would have been his first reaction. They worked silently, taking packs of slates up the scaffold to the roof where the roofers were laying them on with little copper pins and crampons. It was hot and they took their shirts off. There was another ugly welt across Jonas's back.

Just before eleven Chamath said: 'You'd better call them. They were asking about you.'

Jonas pointed silently at his face and a sound escaped him, and if Chamath hadn't known better he would have thought it was a sob.

'At least call and tell them you're not well, you can't come in for another week.'

As it happened there was no work for either of them, and at the end of the day they walked home in silence. Chamath wanted to suggest going out for a drink but something held him back. Instinctively he realized each of them had things they were holding back from the other, things they were ashamed of. They parted at the Harrow Road junction. Chamath stood a long time watching Jonas as he walked on, head bowed and hands in his pockets. Come back, he wanted to shout. You can tell me, I'll understand. As I know you will understand when I tell you my tale. But he didn't. He realized as always that men were not in the habit of unburdening themselves to other men. Whoever said *No man is an island* was wrong. Or perhaps he had meant *woman* when he said *man*.

There was a blue airmail letter on the mat. With a sigh he took it upstairs. The yellow street lamps had come on. He opened the window and stood in the darkness looking out, listening to the street sounds that came through, the distant summer voices of children, the murmur of somebody's TV. And in his mind he was back in that flat in Wimbledon again. What were they doing tonight? Were they sitting there regretting the money they had spent? It was still in his pocket. He half wanted to go back and give it to them. Look, I got as much out of this as you did, so please take it back. Please. I want you to be my friends, not my clients.

It was getting cold. He shut the window and turned on the light, and the moment was gone: he was back in the present. He opened the letter.

My darling boy,

Elsie Pilapitiya has just phoned to say that they will be accompanying the presidential party to the Commonwealth Conference in the Bahamas, and then back through London. They will be there from the 1st to the 10th of next month at Grosvenor House. She would like to meet you to assess your suitability as a prospective husband for her daughter, who I understand is now of a marriageable age.

As you know they are old family friends from a decent Kandyan background. In fact Elsie is distantly related to me on my mother's side. Unlike us, they are *important* people—no doubt you are aware that he is the chef-de-cabinet to the current President. She would like to meet you on Saturday the 2nd at 10 in the morning in their suite. Please be there, and please make sure to be neat and tidy—I know too well how slovenly you can look when you don't make the effort!

On another note, since I have not heard from you I am assuming that no news is good news, that the new tenants have moved in, that the mortgage payments are up to date. I presume that you have now got lodgings, so please send me the address.

In haste,

Your loving Father

Great! thought Chamath, that's all I want. Another agricultural show, another livestock inspection. Maybe she'll get me to strip off too. Maybe she'll want to check out the goods herself to make sure they're in working order. Then he remembered that Saturday was a working day on site. I can't ask Val for yet another half-day's leave, he thought, so I'm afraid that's it. That particular Kandyan princess will have to settle for another bloodline. Not mine.

He thought of the flat still without a tenant. A sudden feeling of danger engulfed him, like a traveller crossing one of those rope bridges in rural Sri Lanka who, against orders, looks down at the foaming river below. And then he looked back up. There was no danger whatsoever of the payments falling behind: there was money coming in, and quite a lot of it too. His career as a *professional* was flourishing.

The monsoon was setting in. There was a thick grey fuzz of weather hanging all day over Galle Road and the noise of traffic came through muffled, as if through a blanket. The typing was not going well. The old man had got to the worst part, he could see the horrors that lay ahead. He could see each and every moment of the future freeze-framed. It was as if each frame had been separately cut out, and the entire block pasted together to form a single instant. For a moment the old man felt like God: he was standing outside of time, watching it as if it were a single, measurable, finite quantity, embedded in the ordinary cubic dimensions of this world. But he was human, not divine. For it to have any meaning at all in human terms, the frames needed to be separated out and attached in sequential order, the film re-run, the life re-lived. Shrugging his shoulders unhappily he pressed on.

At nights when it rained there was an irregular drip, drip from the hole in the roof directly over the bed. It wasn't enough to make the old man move the bed. In fact it was quite invigorating, really, to have your face refreshed in this random manner. Occasionally the old man woke up soaked. But this bed-wetting didn't unduly disturb him. He knew precisely what was wrong: the electrician who drilled the concrete to fix the fan hook had been over enthusiastic and gone right through the slab. No amount of filling the hole with concrete would help now: the water would always find its way through. But the fan was on all night and it worried the old man that it was getting wet. He went downstairs and rang the bell.

'I would like, if I may, to bring an electrician to look at the fan,' he murmured.

'Fan? What's wrong with it?' said Bar. 'You know the wiring was done by Fenton's, the best in the business. Please be careful who you bring in. I wouldn't want any cowboy handyman poking around up there, ruining the high standards of workmanship.'

'I'll be careful,' promised the old man.

'And how's the Revenue Department?'

'Revenue Department?'

'Oh, never mind,' said Bar.

In the meantime, the puppy had given the ladies a new lease of life. All day they could be heard calling out plaintively, 'Shorts, Shorts, where's my lovely Shorts, then? Come to me you naughty, smelly Shorts!'

Every day there was a visit to Ching the vet. There was rabies and worming and parvo. There were ticks to be picked and toenails to be clipped. Shorts was small enough to wriggle with a bit of difficulty through the grill door and escape out into the rain. At any time of day there was at least one sodden landlady and one damp puppy downstairs. The smell of wet dog rose lazily up the staircase and drifted in through the old man's window. He began to dream.

would be sacked without a thought once *their* four months were up.

'Fucking bastards! ' Jonas screamed. There was an edge of hysteria to his voice.

They were sent back to work. It was grouting today and Jonas spent the rest of the day quietly sabotaging his work. He mixed the white cement vigorously with too much water so there were air bubbles in the mixture. After a month of use the grout would snap and crackle like biscuit, leaving the dirt to get in between the tiles. Workmen are like waiters, Chamath thought. Be nice to them. They won't spit in your food; they'll do worse things.

The next day was Friday, their last. Val put them to work on different houses, perhaps for fear of a backlash if they were together. I'll be sorry to leave this, Chamath thought. At the end of the day they were paid unceremoniously. No handshakes, no patting on the back. They walked home together and Chamath realized with a start he wouldn't be seeing Jonas again, that the camaraderie of the building site would be gone.

'Let's go for a drink,' he said. 'We can exchange addresses, keep in touch. We live close by to each other after all.'

Jonas looked at him. His face broke into a smile, clear and luminous, as if that light inside his head had gone on again. 'I don't think so, mate. Nothing personal, it's not about you. This is the way it's always been with me. When you're here every day, you're always in my mind, I think about you a lot. But when you're gone, you're gone.'

He squeezed Chamath's shoulder. 'You'll be all right, mate, don't worry. We did good, didn't we?'

With a cheery wave he walked on down the Harrow Road without once looking back. Chamath watched him go, and even though he couldn't see it he could see it, the ugly welt on Jonas's back, now turned to the colour of mildewed blue grape.

The old man stopped typing and looked up. It was funny how all these people were so alive, so real in his head. Yet they did not now exist, not in the form *his* reality took, and maybe they never had. If they were still alive and he met them now, this instant, they would be older and different—not be the people *he* had known. Would even their memories be the same as his? Perhaps what they had taken away from it all had been quite different to what he took. So who then was the possessor of the ultimate, the absolute truth? You carry your truth with you, he thought, like an ikon slipped in between your heart and your shirt. You don't have to take it out and look at it every minute of the day. The knowledge of it is enough and it is, after all, only an ikon: what is important is what it represents. But don't be fooled for a minute into thinking your ikon is the same as your lover's or your brother's. And don't even stop to think what *that* actually means, because if you did, you would want to slit your wrists. Life would, quite simply, be untenable.

The landladies were rifling through Daddy's record collection.

'Some Kaffringha, dear, that's what we need. Some strong meat.'

They couldn't find any Kaffringha.

Then Ginnie found an album, blue-grey all over, with yellow lettering. 'Will this do? It's by someone called Fela Kuti.'

'Fellow Cootie? What sort of name is that?'

They put it on. The strong clear West African rhythms filled the room.

'Aah, that's more like it.'

The only trouble was it adhered to no known norms of ballroom dancing.

'Freestyle, dear. You over there. Me over here.'

They began dancing, each on her own. Ginnie's hands curled and snaked through the air, conjuring up images of bejewelled maidens in rice paddies, and pristine white dagobas on hill tops.

'No dear, that's *entirely* wrong. Wrong continent. This is how you do it.' Bar began gyrating, her top half stationary, the bottom half moving with a life entirely its own. She was astonishingly competent.

'Bar,' said Ginnie in alarm. 'Bar!'

Too late. Her swirling dérrière had swept the Sacred Heart lamp clean off its stand. There was wax everywhere. The music continued, filling the little parlour with a vibe it hadn't had since Daddy's days. Still the old man failed to appear.

Upstairs he could hear the boom-boom coming up through the floor, and the nasal counterpoint of Fela Kuti's all-woman chorus. Perhaps this is how you do it, he thought. You run your life along a single clear line. The landladies lived still in those heady post-war years when the champagne flowed like ginger beer, and the ginger beer flowed like champagne. Perhaps the ikon they carried was of a ginger beer bottle just opened, the bubbles fizzing, spitting, flaring. Permanently.

The old man guessed that in their lives too there must have been lows as well as highs: but they simply did not exist in the ladies' minds. So who was to say they ever had? I think not, therefore I am not. Or if you want to be clever about it: *I think not, therefore I survive.*

It was strange waking up unemployed, not having anything to do or anywhere to get to in a hurry. For a few moments he felt liberated, free; and then the uneasiness came back, as if he had disobeyed orders again and looked down at the river below. He really did now need to let the flat. Oh, Jamila where are you, he thought with a sort of futile despair. I need your help more than ever. He knew he had to set things right with her: but she hadn't bothered to hide her loathing, the sheer physical disgust she felt for him, and it was as if this had tainted him. He could see himself through her eyes now: this is how a leper must feel when he is cured and rehabilitated, and released back into the normal world; and he still has to deal with the revulsion in people's eyes. But I am not a leper, I am not a pariah. I will get up, get dressed, go down and knock on her door. She is a good woman, she will not refuse to help me.

And then, very conveniently for him because he didn't want to obey these dictates, the thought came to him that he really *did* have somewhere to go, an appointment to get to, that morning at ten. The small matter of being inspected by a Kandyan princess for *marriage-worthiness*. He leapt out of his sleeping bag.

The fourth floor of Grosvenor House was crawling with Sri Lankan security but mention of the magic name Pilapitiya and the crowds parted like waves of the Red Sea. The chef-de-cabinet was in a suite all the way at one end. The door was opened by the elderly Kumarihamy herself.

'You're Raja's son!' she said beaming. 'Come in, come in, let me take a good look at you.'

She led him into a thick-cut deep-pile room, all green, overlooking the Park—the last word in *luxe* and *volupté.*

'The view is not bad, is it?' she said following his eye. 'But these tiny rooms . . . we who live in the countryside . . .' her voice trailed off. Chamath stood obediently under the chandelier while she walked around him, and it was no different from that other livestock inspection which seemed so long ago now.

'Sit,' she finally commanded. Chamath looked round for any evidence of a possibly-soon-to-be bride but there was none. What he did see through an open doorway was an old man seated on the bed, packing what looked like chocolates into an enormous porcelain jar. She saw him looking.

'When we were in Nassau, Fidel invited HE over to Havana for lunch,' she said. 'You know he sent the plane to pick us up? And on the way back, just as we were boarding, he presented us with six jars of chocolates. Six, can you imagine?'

She shook herself out of this glorious reverie. 'Now tell me about yourself. What exactly do you do?'

And then the devil took hold of his tongue. 'I'm a professional,' he said softly.

'Of course you're a professional,' she said, a little irritably. 'I know *that*, but what in?'

'I'm a rent boy.'

She looked nonplussed for a moment. 'Rent boy? Oh, you mean you go around collecting your father's rents, do you? Splendid, *splendid*! Nothing like learning the family business early on.'

She got up abruptly, went over to the desk and came back with a file which she opened. 'I know your father's delicate sensibilities,' she said. 'He will not have told you all this. But I am made of stronger stuff, and I believe in being direct. We will be giving our daughter a *substantial* dowry. You won't of course be getting the Walauwa itself. That goes to our son, naturally, since he will be carrying on the name. But you will get the fields behind it. Then there is *quite* a decent house in Colpetty, and another smaller one in Borella suitable for letting.' She stopped and took a breath. 'Then there are the certificates of deposit, quite a number of them. And something in excess of a million rupees in her current account. But all that is neither here nor there! One look at her and I *know* you'll fall in love.'

As she talked on he was getting more and more agitated. *Is this love or is this commerce?* he wanted to shout. In what way are you different from all those people who currently pay good money for my love? He wanted to spring up and unzip himself. You want substantial? I'll give you substantial. Enough to keep your princess smiling the rest of her life!

But she carried on, blithely unaware of the rage inside his head. 'We'll let your father know our decision when we get back,' she said beaming and patting his head. 'In the meantime, you be a good little rent boy now.'

Cruelly, when he most needed it, there was no work for him, either that evening or the following, Sunday. He walked over the little railway bridge by the school and up to Kensal Rise, past funeral directors and halal butchers, West Indian hairdressers and junk shops. He knew Jonas lived somewhere around here but there was no sign of him either.

Just pick up the phone and call Wimbledon, he ordered himself; but he knew somehow he wouldn't. He had a sort of open-ended, happy-go-lucky fatalism about such things: he felt that that an event could only have serious validity if it occurred by some fortunate accident. It was not in his nature to alter the course of anyone's life, least of all his own. They probably had plans for the weekend anyway. Who knows, they might even have ordered in another professional.

After walking for hours he arrived back at Hiley Road. He must have been fifty yards from the house when he caught sight of her. She had left the house and was walking in the other direction, towards the station. He sprinted.

Panting, he overtook her. 'Jamila, I need to talk to you. Please.'

She looked up, startled.

'They sacked me from the building site. I need to get the flat in order. I need your help. Please.'

He gave her a brilliant smile, the sort of smile that had never failed in the past to warm the stone face of the temple goddess. She didn't slow down and he had to keep pace with her. 'You poor, poor sod,' she said sarcastically. 'Why don't you go ask those rich old women you fuck for some hand-outs?' She quickened her pace and he knew there was no use following. He went back to the empty house.

This question of loneliness was beginning to bother him. He had neither less nor more friends now than he had ever had. So why did he feel so alone? Then the answer came to him. It's the company I keep at night, he thought, the lives of complete strangers I am paid to inhabit, four hours at a time. It's addictive. The more I have the more I need. It's withdrawal symptoms I'm suffering from, not loneliness. And the sex? Is that addictive too? He felt a small stirring. Yes. The sex is addictive too.

It was almost dark when he went back out again to the phone boxes near the station. The phone rang eight times; he was about to put it down when she picked up on the ninth.

'It's me, Norton,' he said, using his professional name.

'You!' she exclaimed.

'Are you doing anything tonight? Can I come round?'

'Where do you live?' she asked curiously. 'What's your real name?'

Without any hesitation he told her.

'Don't move,' she ordered. 'I'll be round to pick you up.'

Hard bastard, he thought. Yeah, right.

He hadn't wanted her to see the inside of his flat, ashamed and afraid she would see it through estate agent eyes. But she insisted on coming up.

'You live here?' she asked, in slight disbelief.

'Yes. Why?'

She didn't answer for a moment. 'You looked, you sounded so respectable. So decent.'

'I *am* respectable, I *am* decent,' he said with a smile.

'Go on, get your things together,' she said briskly. 'You're coming to stay with us in Wimbledon. You can move back once this place is done up. I'm not taking no for an answer.'

He was so full of happiness he wanted to hug her.

But he realized that in this short space of time their relationship had undergone a subtle, indefinable change. He was no longer in charge, no longer the professional. More like a stray dog she had picked up off the streets on a whim.

She drove her black GTI fast, with great precision.

'Just to get one thing clear,' he said. 'This is not for money.'

'Oh, perfectly clear.' She looked at him sideways and grinned. 'You couldn't afford us, anyhow.'

9

Amazing how the look of a place could change when you were no longer there for just work. Perhaps you could let your guard down and observe: how the front door had Victorian stained glass protected by iron mesh on the inside of the panels; how the beige stair carpet continued right on inside the flat, so you almost felt the entire house was yours. It struck him later how in all the time he was there—two months perhaps—he was never to meet any other occupant of the building.

'Where's Stelios?' he asked.

'He'll be coming home late,' she replied.

'Sunday night's an odd night to be coming home late,' he said, and immediately regretted making such a charged statement. He was new to this game of friendship. He must remember to proceed with caution.

They went upstairs and she let him in through the front door of the attic flat. There was a bowl on a small table in the entrance lobby. She fished about in it and pulled out a bunch of keys. 'You'll need these to get in and out,' she said.

How trusting! he thought. This is London, and when you think about it she's only met me once before. Is it because I look so dumb-ass and innocent? Or is it because once you've trusted someone with your body there's nothing more of consequence to risk?

Her name was Elena. Her father the old Marqués was divorced from her mother, a television presenter in Madrid. The father lived on in the castle, farming ten-odd hectares of vineyard which produced a few thousand bottles every year.

'Do you ever get to drink it?' he asked.

'It's what we're drinking now,' she said raising her glass to the light. 'We had some the other night too.'

His eyes couldn't help straying over her while she talked, the perfection of her limbs almost an affront to the absurd dishcloth dress she wore, that was neither short enough to be sexy nor long enough to be elegant.

She had met Stelios at college where they were both studying for a business diploma. 'It was one of those fake colleges that survived on foreign students: rich Colombian girl architects destined never to build anything more than castles in the air; and Greek ship-owners' sons. Stelios—he's from Limassol in Cyprus— was hardly a ship-owner's son. He was only there to keep his student visa alive.' She was silent for a moment. 'Then he met me, we married, and that was that. You know, he hasn't stopped talking about you all week?'

'Well, that's flattering,' he said quietly.

The wine was beginning to take hold of her. 'No really, there's something about you that makes people want to protect you. A little-boy-lost look. For a big guy that's a hard act to pull off. Must be why you're so popular with customers.'

'So it's not for my lovemaking skills, or anything as idiotic as that?'

She looked at him silently for a moment. 'No,' she said.

He was stung by that. The only one you wanted to impress, he thought. The only one who wasn't impressed in the slightest.

She touched his hands with both of hers. 'Oh, I'm sorry, I didn't mean it like that.' She laughed. 'I'm very happy with my husband.'

It was his turn to be silent. 'Then why am I here?'

'For him,' she said softly. 'Though he would die rather than admit that.'

Chamath looked up, shocked. 'You're kidding me, right?'

She shook her head. 'It takes all sorts. You of all people should know that.'

'If you were *my* wife,' he said after a while, 'no way would *I* want to share you with anyone else.'

She smiled. 'Thanks. I'll remember that when the time comes.'

And if there was even a hint of patronization in her voice he was too young to pick it up.

It was past eleven. 'I'm going to lay out the sheets there, under the window,' she said. 'I know you'll be warm enough but I'll leave you a blanket.'

He tried not to let the disappointment show. It was, after all, a new container: he knew from experience that the water would quietly, unobtrusively, assume its shape; in no time at all it would be as if this was how it had always been.

So you go to sleep, then, and dream of home. And in the middle of the night somebody's shaking you awake, roughly. 'She's waiting for you,' he says. Half-asleep you follow him into the bedroom. And you're on top of her now, rising and falling, rising and falling, like that free-fall parachutist in the film, and you feel a man's hand on your shoulder blades like a sign of approval or something, a physical benediction almost. And suddenly you flash past Jamila who seems to be on this free-fall with you, and she zips up to you, her face all be-goggled and scrunched up in the wind, and she mouths the words 'You disgust me,' then she zips away again. And you don't really care at all because the wind is all around you and you're falling. Falling.

In the morning he sat across from her sipping the pale Earl Grey that always tasted to him of mild soap suds, and the sun came in through the window filling him with happiness. They might have been an old married couple; except that a married couple would not have been this happy.

Stelios had gone to work.

'What does he do?' Chamath asked curiously.

'Don't laugh,' she said. 'He works at the London Foot Hospital in Fitzroy Square.' Then she laughed. 'He works in the basement dispensary. It's full of fellow Cypriots, he loves it. And you?'

He told her about the building site and how he had just been sacked. They didn't talk about his visa. She had figured him out now, and the unspoken assumption lay between them: he was one of those creatures who lived below the grid, in the blue-grey twilight world occupied by illegals.

'What you need is a good Spanish wife,' she said finally. 'I have my best friend in Madrid—she's single— her name is Luz.'

I really don't want any best friend of yours called Luz, he thought. I want you. But he smiled politely and said nothing.

She finished her tea and got up. 'I can drop you at Kensal Green if you like. I pass that way to work.'

In the car she said, 'I'll be back by six. Will you be home then?'

He shrugged. 'Depends. If I have to work tonight or not.'

When he opened his door there was a folded piece of paper slipped under it. Jamila's list of people to call. He took it downstairs and knocked on her door. But she must have already gone to work. He went back up to his flat. There was a cold in the air he hadn't noticed before, as if the place had been uninhabited a long time, as if his spirit, his soul, had already packed its bags and left. He looked at the alien blue of the bathtub, the yellow turmeric stain on the worktop shrieking in a language he now found totally foreign. He thought: It really didn't take long, did it, for me to change my allegiance and jump ship? He felt more than ever like the garbage-feeding rat Jamila was making him out to be.

There was a thin rain falling when he went back out to the telephone box. They had a job for him that night in Central London, an all-nighter if he wished. I won't go back to Wimbledon when I finish, he thought, it'll be too late and I can't disturb them at that hour. I will stay here and make an effort to sort out this flat. I will show Jamila that I am strong enough to carry the weight of my own troubles.

In the late nineteenth century the land at the bottom of the garden had been acquired to build the railway to

Galle, and a century later more for the Marine Drive. This was where the local populace went to meet and greet, to take the sea air and exercise. Bar and Ginnie had never ventured this far. It was not fitting for any *lady*, let alone a Ginger Beer Princess, to be seen walking on a public road. But sacrifices have to be made, and in the interests of curbing the boisterousness of Shorts the landladies decided to take the plunge.

There was just one problem. What to wear? They rooted about in what they liked to call their dressing room—pulling out woollen tights and tasselled handbags, antique toques and tasteful tea gowns; even a tiara set with Matara diamonds. (Oh look, Ginnie, remember how we sacked Kanthi for stealing Mummy's tiara? Well here it is! You know, I'm sure that crafty girl sneaked right back in one night to replace it?) But they could find no tracksuits.

'I hear they do very good ones at the Mouse of Passion,' said Bar. 'Very cheap.'

'Bar, how could you! The Mouse is only for tourists and returnees. Besides, what would Daddy say?'

That settled it. They went to Odel instead.

'Be sure to wrap up warm, dear. I hear it's very cold in there.'

Ginnie wore her silver fox stole. She had last worn it when Daddy's horse (Carbon Dioxide) came second in the Governor's Cup at Nuwara Eliya. They went up the escalator, shedding quite a lot of silver fox as they went. To the left of the escalator overlooking the atrium was an enormous blown-up photo of a palm-fringed beach with a bikini-clad model on it.

'Oh look, dear. I suppose that's been put there to make us feel warm.'

The sales assistant watched them rising up the escalator, in a mounting state of excitement. She had read about people like this in history class. They were called *Victorians.*

'Could you direct us to hosiery, dear?'

The assistant was tongue-tied, unused to being in the company of famous people. Also, she didn't know what 'hosiery' meant.

'Millinery, then? Or how about *haberdashery*?'

They finally found their way to tracksuits. Bar chose a midnight blue one with sequins. Ginnie's was a *miris-malu* red.

'Red, dear? Won't you be sending out the wrong signals in that?'

'And what sort of signals might those be?'

'Well, *you* know. Him. Doesn't that colour rather scream *Come and get me, I'm all yours?*'

'Really, Bar, what a nasty mind you have. I thought we had definitely agreed that he is a convicted sex-offender who's had his tackle removed to curb his urges?'

'Tackle? *Tackle?* Who's got a nasty mind now?'

Back home there was a strange man in their front

garden in flashy yellow rubber slippers, with a perfectly rounded belly that poked out of a tee shirt that was too short.

'You see!' hissed Bar.

'I don't know,' said Ginnie. 'What *do* I see?'

'Does that look like a tax inspector to you?'

Ginnie had to agree it didn't.

'He's obviously a fellow sex-offender. Can't you just smell the air of depravity about him?'

'I don't know,' said Ginnie doubtfully. 'He doesn't look very capable to *me*.'

It was, in fact, the old man's electrician, who would have been mortified to hear that last comment.

Once inside, the ladies realized they were too tired to take the dog anywhere.

'Some music, I think, dear. How about that Fellow?'

'Fela, Bar. *Fela*!'

'I know, dear. You don't have to get all American on *me*.'

The music coloured and scented the room, rising like wood smoke to the floor above. The old man breathed in and dreamed.

10

Eaton Terrace, one of the most beautiful streets in London, and your josephine—deep-voiced and authoritative—sitting in her chocolate-coloured drawing room with baroque gilt mirrors on every wall and a washed-silk, Chinese Tientsin rug on the floor.

'I thought we'd slum it tonight in Soho,' she says. 'You like Chinese?' You nod because you've eaten in those holes-in-the-wall most of your working life (*won ton noodle soup, fifty pence*) and it is only a home away from home for you.

And before you go you ask to use the loo and she follows you in shutting the door behind her, and it is so small in there you have her up against the door, one foot on the lid of the closed lavatory pan, the other on the floor, and you think of that old-style Hollywood sex where one foot must never leave the floor and you're pleased you've been able to comply. And the door goes *bang-bang-bang*—it must be plywood—and you think, this door sounds awfully cheap for a posh place like this, doesn't it?

And afterwards she takes you to Soho, to a restaurant in Lisle Street all green with a dirty great blown-up photo of a beach with palm trees and you think, She's taking me to dinner in Sri Lanka, how nice of her! But just before you enter you notice a guy standing all alone in the dark alley by the side of the restaurant, leather jacket, white shirt, dark trousers, and those watchwords *discreet* and *good-looking* come to mind; and when your eyes travel up to his face you realize he's smiling at you, a slightly cynical smile in the curve of his lips, and you know he's sussed out exactly who and what you are, and you smile back because you've sussed out exactly who and what *he* is. And in those bitter-sweet, world-weary smiles you exchange you wish each other all the goddam luck in the world, in this age-old battle between rich and poor, white and brown, old and young. Because it's not your fault you've both been born to the wrong side, the side that will always lose.

And inside she orders a giant crab in ginger and spring onion, and when the waiter puts down the dish she says in a loud voice for all of Soho to hear, 'You know, your come is running down my leg?' and the waiter scuttles off in fright, and you swear even the crab is blushing pink with embarrassment.

And back home because the bedroom is just too far

away—or because she just doesn't want to spoil the sheets, who knows?—she pushes you down on the floor and mounts you roughly and repeatedly, riding you all the way to Sloane Square and back. And it is only next day you realize you have carpet burn all across your buttocks and the backs of your ankles. Damned Chinese, you think. Couldn't they wash their rugs a bit better?

There was a white haze hanging over the sea at sunset, giving the evening walkers a backlit, surreal look. One man walked with both arms outstretched, like an old-fashioned sleepwalker in a silent film. Another ran backwards with strange hopping movements. Every once in a while he toppled off the red brick path into the oncoming traffic. The red white and blue evening trains flashed by, laden with onlookers, open-mouthed at this brazen spectacle of the rich and famous at play. Then there were the tracksuits. Oh, the tracksuits!

'I think, dear, those sequins were a wise choice. They hit absolutely the right note.'

'Thank you dear. Wish I could say the same about that red.'

Shorts ran wildly, joyously, pulling the landladies along on their lead. It gave him such pleasure to see them so limbered up, so exercised; and at times so airborne. They were a magnet for various elderly gents walking their own dogs.

'Oh look at that magnificent harlequin beast over there!'

'And the dog's not bad either.'

'Shh, I think he's coming over. Pretend you haven't seen him.'

'Good evening ladies. Do you need any help with that puppy? He's quite frisky, isn't he?'

'Is he?' said Bar frostily. 'He's not the only one, I fear. A very good evening to you!' Turning round smartly she walked off in the opposite direction.

'What did you do that for?' asked Ginnie, trotting to catch up with her.

'I told you the red was trouble.' They headed up the lane for home. 'It's a good thing it's dark,' said Bar. 'We can sneak you in without Him seeing.'

The electrician had been less than useless. 'Very, very difficult job,' he said shaking his head from side to side.

'No it isn't,' snapped the old man irritably. 'All I'm asking is for you to move the fan to another point, and block up the hole with some concrete.'

'The Perehara,' said the electrician.

The Perehara was a religious parade in Kandy, an annual affair.

'I'm taking the wife to Kandy for the Perehara.'

'But that's in a month's time!'

'Precisely. I can come to you in August, once I get back.'

'I'll call you if I can't find anyone else.' In disgust, the old man went out and spent the afternoon at the Mouse of Passion. The urge to be a builder again made his fingers twitch, bringing back memories. So he wasn't able to resist the ready-made curtains in their pack. On the way back he stopped at a hardware store and bought curtain hooks and rings, brackets and concrete nails. They didn't have curtain poles but they had broom handles for sale, minus the broom heads. That would have to do. He took the lot back and spent a happy couple of hours of DIY.

The ladies returned to be confronted by this new development. The old man's window had a curtain drawn across it, obscuring the inside completely. His light was on and it shone through, mellow and inviting, making the curtains glow. A warm *come-and-get-me-I'm-all-yours* sort of red.

'Well,' said Bar. '*Well!*'

Chamath spent the morning in the telephone box. Nobody could come then and there (*Who do you think I am, mate, Stirling Moss?*) so he fixed appointments for later on in the week. Carpet fitters and plumbers, and a roofer to look at the damp patch above the bedroom window. He decided to do the painting himself. At eleven he was still in the box, and was almost relieved when Gary said there was no work for him that evening.

He went off to Kensal Rise to the second-hand shops, and on a wild spending spree—there was no stopping him now—he bought two single beds, almost new, at fifteen pounds apiece, a fiver for delivery. He got them home and up the stairs; they filled the bedroom entirely. Never mind, he thought, it's only for tenants. In the afternoon he visited Mr Shafeeq at the corner shop. He bought a chicken and a kilo packet of Basmati rice, onions, garlic and ginger, cloves and cardamoms.

'Cooking dinner for the girl?' Mr Shafeeq asked.

'What girl?'

Mr Shafeeq smirked. 'I seen you with her. Black bird. Big red hair. Big knockers.'

'They say Idi Amin's escaped,' Chamath said in ruthless retaliation. 'They say he's coming to live in Kensal Green.'

Mr Shafeeq turned a whiter shade of pale.

Chamath showed him the shopping basket. 'What vegetables?' he demanded.

'Take the okra,' said Mr Shafeeq nervously. 'And make a tomato salad with coriander leaves.'

It wasn't often Chamath cooked Indian but when he

did, Mr Shafeeq was his menu planner. In another life he might have been a dietician or health guru.

At the door Chamath turned back to look at him sternly. 'She's not my girl,' he said.

'Yeah, right,' said Mr Shafeeq grinning.

He let himself into the empty Wimbledon flat and breathed in the warmth, the all-brown-ambience of his new home, and his spirits lifted on the wings of this quiet contentment. He was frying the onions and spices together with the turmeric, chilli and curry powder when he heard the key in the door and felt a familiar hand on his shoulder.

'What I love most,' said Stelios hoisting himself up on the counter-top. 'Watching other people work.'

'How was your day?'

'Not bad. You must come round to Fitzroy Square and meet the gang. You'd have a lot in common.'

Chamath put in the cut chicken pieces and turned up the gas.

'You know we were really worried when you didn't turn up last night? We were afraid we'd done something to upset you.'

Chamath smiled at him, his face flushed with the heat of the frying. By the time Elena came home the curry was cooked, and they had almost finished the bottle Chamath had brought.

'Much better than *your* wine, doll,' Stelios said kissing his wife.

'So, nobody's forcing you to drink mine,' she replied good-naturedly.

They sat down to eat. 'Tell us about last night,' she said.

Chamath shook his head and grinned. 'I got carpet burn all across my backside.'

'You poor baby, you want Mummy to rub some cream on it?'

But they knew they were on dangerous ground, and instinctively the conversation veered back to everyday topics. At the end of the evening, she presented him with the folded sheets from the linen cupboard and he took them obediently, making up his nest under the window. He woke up briefly in the early hours, dimly aware that there had been no urgent summons that night, no hand shaking him awake. You have to choose, he said to himself sternly, between their love and their sex. You know perfectly well you can't have both. And so saying, he turned over and went back to sleep.

11

'So you see, it's always been me and her,' your josephine is saying.

You're sitting in Rowley's, Jermyn Street, looking at the mirrors, the tiles, the sanded floorboards; but actually you're miles away, up in an attic south of the river. *Concentrate!* you say to yourself. *You have a job to do here, fucker!*

'She's been part of my life for as long as I can remember. I wake up with her, I go to bed with her.'

At the words *go to bed with her* your ears prick up. This could be an interesting night.

'Who?' you ask hopefully. 'Your best friend?'

'No, you silly!' she gives you an arch look. 'My *vaginismus*. How many times do I have to explain? Oh, you hire-guys you're all the same. Only one thing on your mind, get in there quick as you can. Wham-bam-thank-you-ma'am. Well, not this time, buster, *not this time!*'

Your heart sinks at this. 'So you've done this before?'

She gives a little self-satisfied sigh, putting her thick blond hair back into a knot, crossing her chunky thighs under the table to the juicy sound of silken stockings rubbing up against each other. '*Dozens* of times. Never works. When I saw your picture I thought, ah, Indian. Perhaps a touch of the Ayurveda will do the trick. And you've heard of tantric sex, but Ayurvedic sex? That's something new! The steak arrives and you tuck in because you know you have a long night ahead. She looks at your plate. 'You know it's horse?' she says, and you almost choke. 'I'm Italian, I was in the restaurant trade, I can always spot horse.' She looks at you meaningfully from under her black eyebrows. 'Horse is good for a man; if you get my drift.'

It's a long trek up to Finchley, to a long tall house on a quiet road, with a shimmering phosphorescence in the garden—an empty swimming pool.

'For my husband,' she says. 'I don't bother filling it up now. Can't afford to, anyway.'

'Husband?' you ask in alarm.

'Don't worry.' She grips your arm. 'He went out with the first heart attack. I sold the sandwich bar then. I give out rooms now to make ends meet.'

Then she answers the question you didn't have the courage to ask. 'No,' she says, 'he didn't manage either. We tried and tried.' She sighs. 'In the end we had to think of other ways to enjoy ourselves.'

'So it was a blessed relief, then, when he went?'

She shoots you a look. Humour is not her strong suit. You have a sudden vision of the swimming pool full, the husband's body floating upside down in it. The Victim of Vaginismus.

She opens the front door and you follow her into the hall. And as if on cue a downstairs door opens and a little man pops out.

'Ah, Giovanna,' he says. 'I see you've brought back another of your young friends.'

'Goodnight, Brian,' she says firmly. 'Don't mind him,' she whispers. 'He's always trying to get into my knickers.' And you wonder whether to believe her. And up the stairs on the first landing the bedroom has a kidney-shaped dressing table with frilly pink pleats round it, and a white-painted curly-wurly iron bed: a femininity strangely at odds with your josephine, who has heavy solid limbs typical of the southern part of the peninsula. You have a vision of her in black headscarf, her big feet with their splayed toes mercilessly crushing grapes; and other things.

She strips voluptuously, and you almost feel you're in a film by Fellini. 'Down you go,' she says in a sing-song voice, spreading her legs wide. 'Nothing will happen till I'm relaxed.'

Experience has taught you that in these cases relaxation is next to impossible, especially with a complete stranger you're paying by the hour. But you don't say this, because the customer is never wrong. She settles in, putting her arms behind her head, smiling with complicit complacence at the ceiling which has no doubt been privy to many such previous episodes. And you find in spite of everything you're rather enjoying yourself—the vitamin-enriched, gunmetallic taste of her nub a fitting end to the steak dinner. But every time you come up for air she pushes you back down, firmly, her thighs tight around your head, and you think of grapes being crushed. (And other things.)

And when your time is up and the gates haven't yet opened—as you expected—she says almost victoriously, 'There, I *told* you!' And you know it is almost a point of honour with her that she should not have succeeded.

'I should ask for my money back, shouldn't I,' she says fondly, 'for non-performance?'

You don't answer because by now you realize your tongue is probably damaged beyond repair. You may *never* be able to speak again. And who, oh who, will hire a professional with a speech impediment?

'What's the matter?' she says. 'Cat got your tongue?'

Honey, not just any old cat, you want to reply. One *special* pussy.

But you hold your tongue because you remember what that wise man said. Discretion is always the better part of cunnilingus. And you hobble home mildly annoyed because you've been up all night, and she

didn't even have the good manners to take you in hand
for all those man-hours you so bravely put in.

'You want foam-backed or hessian? Wilton or
Axminster? Nylon or wool? Or maybe wool mixed
with nylon?'

'I want,' said Chamath, who had a little difficulty
speaking this morning, 'the cheapest thing going.'

'I can give you cord,' said the man doubtfully. '£1.50
a yard. But I warn you the dirt gets stuck in between
the grooves.'

'That'll be the tenant's dirt then, not mine.'

'What colour?'

'Beige,' said Chamath uncompromisingly. 'The most
neutral beige you have.'

He signed up and paid the deposit. 'I'll call you
when the painting's done. Give me a week.'

Then he went out and bought paint. *Disco*, 1.99
a gallon, colour *mushroom* (beige in other words).
He bought rollers and brushes, overalls and a pair
of aluminium steps, watching his money disappear
with pleasure. He had just dumped everything in the
entrance hall when the downstairs door opened.

'Look,' he said beaming, like a child showing off
his new rollerblading skills. Her face softened for an
instant. She mumbled something—it sounded like

'good'—then she closed her door again.

He carefully stored everything upstairs and locked the door. At 5.30 sharp he was in Fitzroy Square. The London Foot Hospital was in one corner, a splendid Regency building far too grand for mere feet. Stelios introduced him to his departing fellow workers: Artemios and Elpida and Kalavazides from Cyprus; and Zos from Rhodes.

'Great bunch of people,' said Stelios looking fondly at their retreating backs. 'Don't know what I'd do in London without them.' He turned to Chamath. 'So. Are you ready?'

'Ready for what?'

'To hit the gym, dummy.'

They went to the gym where Stelios was still a member, in Clapham where they had lived till they bought the Wimbledon flat.

'Hi Pat, brought you a new customer,' Stelios said breezily.

The woman at the counter looked doubtfully at Chamath. 'You'll have to do the induction course, love. Can't use the gym till you've been shown how to use the machines.'

'I'll give him all the induction he needs,' said Stelios with a wink. 'Leave it to me.'

Chamath filled out the form and paid his membership.

'Your friend's here,' said the woman to Stelios.

'Who? Meg?'

They went inside and Stelios lent him some of his own kit to wear. Meg was at the lats machine and they joined her.

'Is this your brother?' she asked. 'Looks a lot like you.' She had a soft, almost goofy smile, and eyes that looked above and beyond you when she talked, relatively uncorrupted, not fully conversant in the sophisticated language of the big city. School of Constance, Chamath thought; about two years behind. Her short hair was all mussed up and she wore a T-shirt that ended above her belly button, with large holes for arms. Every time she raised them Chamath got an eyeful.

'Now *that* is what I call a real English rose,' Stelios said under his breath, a little wistfully.

Chamath wanted to point out that he had a perfectly decent wife at home; but it wasn't in his position to express an opinion, especially now. He thought of himself, scornfully: You're like a stray dog they've thrown a bone to. You're theirs for life now. And I hate to say this, you're a little in love with them both, aren't you? And what's wrong with that? answered the other voice in his head. Why can't you love people out of a sense of loyalty and gratitude and duty? He thought sadly: if they asked you today to jump off a cliff you probably would; and he despised himself, even though he knew there was nothing he could do about it.

It was past eight.

'Shouldn't we be going home?' he asked.

'What's the hurry? There's time for a quick one, isn't there?'

'But Elena?'

'Oh, she knows where to find me,' Stelios said. 'She knows my movements.'

They went to the Windmill on Clapham Common where Stelios ordered a pint of special brew and a half of fresh orange juice for each of them, and they went outside. There were cars moving at the edge of the common and cutting across it, little pin-points of light.

'Did you know her long, before you married?' Chamath asked.

Stelios's eyes followed the cars in the distance. 'I met her first day in college. Somehow I knew that day itself she was the one for me. We feel so right together, you know? We got married a couple of months later.' They were interrupted by a noisy group at the next table singing Happy Birthday and Stelios sang along with them for a bit. 'The thing about Elena is that she's good for me,' he said. 'Keeps me in check, doesn't let me get out of hand.'

'But love? What about love?' Chamath persisted.

'Ah, yes. Love.' Stelios grinned. 'That is something you only find when you're not looking for it.' His eyes bored into Chamath and Chamath looked away. 'Sometimes you have to lose it to understand that it was what you actually had. Though that is not something I expect a young bloke like you to understand.' He paused. 'And you? Anyone special in your life?'

Chamath smiled ruefully. I was only ever a participant in other people's lives, he wanted to say. I never had the luxury or pleasure of living in my own. But he was shy to say all this. These were strangers after all, he didn't know them well enough. It would be self-indulgent and sympathy-seeking: the dog asking for more love, yet another bone. He was not ready to lose those last shreds of self-respect yet.

It was almost eleven when they got home. Elena had already gone to sleep, the bedroom door shut, a not-so-subtle signal that proclaimed *not tonight, thanks*. Stelios pulled him by the hand. 'Come in,' he whispered urgently. 'I know she'd want you to.' But Chamath shook his head. He had a sense of something going on between those two: an invisible charge, a crackle on the line. Instinctively he felt he had no place in the middle of it. His loyalties were equally divided, straight down the middle; he was not ready yet to have to choose. He went to the linen cupboard and got out his sheets.

12

'There's an enquiry for a shoot tomorrow,' Mike said. 'You interested?' Chamath hesitated, thinking of Jonas. 'It's fifty quid, for a cover. Some mag called *After Hours*. They'll need you for two, three hours max.'

Fifty quid! he thought. As much as an all-nighter for a whole lot less work. 'Yeah, all right,' he said.

Mike gave him an address in the far, far north of London, at the outer edges where the town has virtually become countryside. 'It'll take you at least an hour to get there,' he warned. 'Be there ten o'clock sharp.'

He went back to his painting. At the end of the day he used thinner to get the paint off his fingers as best as he could, hung his overalls on the steps and got into his jeans. At the front door he met Jamila coming in.

'I've begun,' he said brightly. 'You must come and see.'

But her mind was elsewhere. 'I'll come up tomorrow,' she said absently, and closed the door.

The landladies jostled about in the forecourt under the mango tree in their newly acquired hunting pinks. Any moment now you expected Sakuntala to come out with a silver tray of stirrup cups and a horn to blow. Suddenly the front gate unlatched and the two ladies charged out at the end of Shorts's lead. You could hear them halooing and braying to the neighbours as they galloped off down to the sea. The old man breathed in the silence—the calm that hung, quivering gently, in the leaves of the mango tree.

Down at the Marine Drive, Bar and Ginnie took in the sea air; or rather the rain, because it was raining.

'I thought you brought the umbrella?'

'I thought *you* brought the umbrella?'

'I had the dog to think of. I can't think of everything.'

Suddenly a very large gent materialized by their side, holding onto a Great Dane and an even greater umbrella with black and white checks. 'Ladies, if I may be permitted?'

Too late Bar recognized the walker from the other day. She briefly considered refusing the kind offer and striking out with the dog in the rain, but she knew Ginnie would never leave such welcome shelter in this fierce monsoon weather. (Lazy cow, she never had principles when you wanted her to have principles.)

A little while later the old man saw from upstairs this strange cavalcade coming in through the gate.

'Won't you come in?' he heard Ginnie say. 'Nothing like a warm cup of Milo on an afternoon like this. Then again, we can do tea? Coffee? Or I know, how about a hot arrack toddy with lime and sugar?' Her voice sounded breathless and fluttery.

The old man noticed with some satisfaction that the old geezer going in through the door downstairs was virtually bald, quite a rough specimen. Jealousy, he thought. Do I detect a tiny note of jealousy here?

So it's a new departure for you then, this shoot business. You take the tube—which quickly turns into a train—to one of those dreary overground stations smelling of damp concrete and piss in the wilds of north London; you find your way after many wrong turns to the studios.

Studios, did you say? Ha! It's the garage attached to somebody's house, cement floors, and a crappy grey roller door that opens with an asthmatic wheeze to reveal a whole sad world of shabby sexual gadgetry, a sort of low-tech love manufactory. There's a set of lights manned by a podgy, good-natured bloke in specs, and the photographer is this old boy (the sort that wears navy blue blazers and Daks slacks, you know the type I mean?) with liver spots on his hands and bum-fluff hair.

Here, drink this, he says, it'll help you relax. Go on it's a margarita, don't be afraid. And there's not much in this triangular glass so you swallow it down because you don't want to appear rude. We pay you once we're sure we got the pictures we want, he says, fifty quid, cash in the hand. And this is irregular, surely, nobody told you about being paid after, but you also see their point, and anyway they're two old fat geezers and you know you can take them both on if there's trouble.

And now you begin to realize there was more in the drink than you bargained for because there's things happening in the downstairs department and the photographer and his assistant are delighted, and they breathe hotly over you as they rearrange you and your bits in the shapes they require. Don't open your eyes so wide, they say. And for God's sake put some life into them. Don't look at the lens, they say. Look just above it. And in no time at all it's a wrap. Time flies, don't it, they say, when you're enjoying yourself?

And surprise, surprise, you get your fifty quid cash in the hand. How old are you? they say. Seventeen? Eighteen? Holland's the place for you, they say. You could make a fortune over there, young boy like you. And you think (unkindly because they've been good enough to pay you cash in hand), Yes, I'd like to go to

Holland with a machine gun and exterminate the lot of you. Fucking paedos.

Harry and I would be delighted, says the old geezer, delighted if you would join us for more margaritas and something to eat. Margaritas? Ha! You would rather have lunch with Hitler's mother and Stalin's aunt. So you pocket your fifty quid and get the hell out, back to the piss-smelling station, back to civilization. And you keep repeating this mantra to yourself as you and your fifty quid bounce along inside the carriage to the sound of the train wheels:

A paedo a day keeps the mortgage away,
A paedo a day keeps the mortgage at bay.

That afternoon he couldn't somehow get back down from the high he was on. He looked fondly at his paintwork lit by the uncompromising afternoon sun. There were patches everywhere. It'll be all covered by the second coat, he thought confidently. All you need in life is a good second coat.

He heard the key turning in the lock and crashed downstairs, taking two steps at a time. 'Come up,' he said. 'Come and see my handiwork.'

She smiled in spite of herself at his enthusiasm. She click-clacked around his flat without saying anything, and he followed holding his breath, waiting for her approval, not daring to hope.

'Well, it's a start,' she said finally, and he let out his breath with relief.

'Tomorrow I start on the woodwork, undercoat. The day after, the second coat of emulsion on the walls. The day after that, the final coat of gloss on the wood . . .'

But he could see she wasn't listening. 'Jamila, is anything the matter?' he asked anxiously.

'No,' she said, turning to go. She stopped at the door. 'I'm cooking stew tonight, you want to come?'

But he thought of the dreariness of downstairs, the TV on at a constant monotone, the aged sofa with the lumps in it. And he thought of Wimbledon, the all-beige flat warm as toast.

'I'm sorry,' he said. 'I made plans.'

'What?' she asked suspiciously. 'You're not still . . . ?'

'Oh no, it's not that.' He made it sound as if *that* were a thing of the past, as if *that* had been just a passing phase. 'It's some friends. I promised I'd go round for a meal.'

'Oh,' she said. She didn't sound convinced. She closed the door on him without another word, and he could hear her weary descent down the stairs.

He went to Willesden High Road, the closest big shopping centre to him and bought a duck and a bottle of champagne. Never mind the mortgage, there'd be plenty more where that came from.

13

'You know all about us,' Elena said. 'We hardly know anything about you.'

'Not much to tell,' he replied after a pause. 'I've been here since the age of eleven—school, university, all that. I don't have a visa to stay any more but I want to stay on.'

'Why?'

'Actually I don't really know.' He shrugged. 'There's only my dad back there. Two aunts. I don't think I really fit in, you know?'

'Are you happy here?'

He smiled at her. 'Now I am.' He was too embarrassed to continue so he got up and went into the kitchen. The duck was singing merrily on the stove. He was braising it with garlic and herbs; he gave it a stir.

'Where did you learn to cook?' she asked curiously.

'By starving,' he said simply. 'It sharpens your wits. It gives you a good instinct for what goes with what.

I'm a naturally greedy person,' he added. 'That helps.'

They sat there getting tipsy, waiting for Stelios, and it was after nine when he got home.

'You could have come to the gym,' he said looking accusingly at Chamath. 'Why didn't you come?'

Chamath saw him through an alcoholic haze. Because I prefer to sit here with your wife, he wanted to say. Actually, if it's all the same to you, I'd prefer to fuck your wife. And then he thought: I don't mean that. You're both my friends; I owe my happiness to *both* of you. He went to the fridge and brought out the champagne.

'So what are we celebrating then?' Stelios asked.

He told them about progress on the flat. Then he outlined his crazy plan for selling the flat, using the money to buy a derelict house to convert. 'I've done the maths,' he said. 'A converted flat sells for virtually the same price as a derelict two-storey house. So your profit is 100 per cent less the conversion cost.'

'You've lost me there,' Stelios said.

He explained: 'An old house in a shitty area would cost in the region of 20,000 quid. Each flat would sell for about 20,000 quid. So your profit is 20,000 less the conversion cost.'

'Which would be?'

'I reckon I could do it for five thousand.'

'Come on then, what are we waiting for?' said Stelios. 'Take me to a shitty area! We can do this together,' he said getting excited, 'you and me. How about it?'

So they drank more Rioja because the champagne was finished, and made their fortunes right there and then under the roof of that beige Wimbledon flat; because they were all under thirty and it's a well-known fact—oh, very well known—that if you don't make your fortune by the time you hit thirty, you'll never make it.

The old man stopped typing. Today was Sakuntala's day and he had to make sure the manuscript was safely under lock and key. She was very bright, very sharp. It would be the work of a moment for her to take it downstairs for the landladies to see. And then where would he be?

At first it had been something of a pain to vacate his room once a week for Sakuntala, especially with the rains steadily getting worse. But as time went on he found more and more that he looked forward to these weekly outings, lasting an hour or so (because that was all it took for Sakuntala to float over his belongings with a duster, thoroughly disarranging his effects: not so much to clean them, but to signal to him that cleaning had been uppermost in her mind when she passed through). Sakuntala's housework was strangely like justice itself: more important that it was seen to be done than to actually *be* done.

This morning he had decided to check out Marine Drive for himself. For weeks the landladies had been yapping at his heels, entreating him to join them; but the old man was a cautious creature; he liked to reconnoitre the terrain first. He was bowling along smartly down to the sea when he heard a voice behind him.

'I say, I say!' it said. '*I say!*'

It was the sort of dated phrase Ginnie's father might have used back in the Ginger Beer era. There was only one person who might use it now. The old man turned round in exasperation and his guess proved correct; it was the harlequin beast from yesterday, still enormous, though somewhat visually imbalanced today without the dog by his side. The slope of the road didn't help either, and it looked as if he might tip over any minute.

'You're the gent that lives above Ginevra's garage.'

So it's *Ginevra* now, is it? the old man wanted to say sharply. Who is she to you?

'I thought I would enlist your help, since you live with them,' said the harlequin beast. He chuckled. 'Though not in *that* sense, obviously.'

'Obviously,' replied the old man coldly.

'You see, I've had my eye on that little lady these last few months. I live over there,' said the Beast, pointing to a hideous sixties block of flats across the road. 'I know, stunning, isn't it? And guess what, it has *an elevator*!' He sounded surprised and gratified that such luxuries existed in the Third World. 'I haven't introduced myself, have I? I'm Don,' he said, rhyming it with *done*. Actually I'm Dananjaya, but back in Antioch, California, they call me Don.'

'I'm sure they do,' said the old man acidly.

'I retired here to *Surrey Lanka* a few months back, and how I love it! The colourful vegetables! The salty breezes!'

Don't they have vegetables and salt in Antioch? the old man wanted to ask, but restrained himself with difficulty. Instead he said, 'So what did you do there?'

'Oh, I was a tailor,' said the beast. 'I covered chairs and sofas. I was really good at my job, I made a fortune!'

The Tailor of Antioch, the old man thought. Like *The Professional of Kensal Green*. How we all end up here, washed up on this coast when we're really no good for anything else!

'. . . so I was thinking maybe you could put in a good word?' The beast thrust a piece of paper into the old man's hand. 'Will you give this to her? It's my number. And I think you and I have a lot to say to each other. We must keep in touch. Let's do lunch one of these days.'

I would rather have lunch with Hitler's mother and Stalin's aunt, the old man thought. But he didn't say it. Instead, he smiled frostily and continued his way down to the sea.

He shared a pot of tea with Elena before she drove him back. This was the time of day he liked best, when the complicated dynamics of a three-way relationship simplified to a two-way one. The rules were more straightforward, he felt more in control.

'At the rate I'm going,' he said enthusiastically, 'the flat will be ready in no time. I can move back then.' He looked at her covertly to see her reaction.

'Why?' she asked. 'Aren't you happy with us?'

'What do you think?'' he said, and wondered if she could see the glorious, delirious happiness in his face.

'Well then. Let's have no more talk of moving out.'

He had a sudden urge to ask: *What exactly do you see in me? What purpose do I actually serve by being here?* But he'd had the great good fortune to be invited to this banquet; he didn't question it for fear it would be taken away. Young as he was, he knew people often did things simply because they felt at the time it was the right thing to do. The 'motives' came later: when the policeman who manned your mind demanded a valid reason, a logical explanation for the absurdity of your behaviour.

At Hiley Road she wanted to come in and inspect the work. She saw the patchy first coat of emulsion, she saw his overalls making their statement on the steps in the middle of the room: an installation entitled *Work in Progress*.

'I'm proud of you,' she said, hugging him. He tried

to hold on to her but she broke free. 'I must go, I'm late for work.'

He followed her downstairs to the front door. 'By the way,' she said. 'You know all that talk last night about Stelios going into partnership with you to convert houses? Don't even think of it.'

'Why?' he asked puzzled.

'He'll come in all enthusiastic because that's the way he is. But he'll lose interest just as quickly. And when you most need him he won't be there.'

She must have seen the shocked look on his face because she continued quickly: 'Oh, he's my husband, I love him dearly. But I know him better than anyone else in the world.' She looked at him with her liquid eyes and sighed. 'I wouldn't want anything bad to happen to you. Stelios has a way of destroying what he loves best, what is most dear to him.' To make up for her words she reached up and kissed him full on the lips, a long lingering kiss. Then she slammed the door shut and was gone. It was only when he turned round that he realized the door to downstairs was open.

'Morning!' he said brightly and went back up.

He began work on the big bay window in the front room overlooking the street: sanding, filling, sanding again. They're only tenants, he kept saying to himself, they're only tenants. Then he began the undercoat, cutting in, cutting out, moving sashes up and down to paint the bits concealed between them. He was on the window sill when Mr Shafeeq walked past, puffing nervously on a cigarette.

'Hi there!' Chamath called out cheerily. 'Why aren't you in the shop?'

'It's Idi Amin,' said Mr Shafeeq. 'Just saw him on TV.' He shivered. 'He's alive! Living in Saudi.'

'Thanks for letting me know,' Chamath said. 'I'll cancel my trip straightaway!' But Mr Shafeeq had scurried off, in no mood for jokes.

There was no work that evening so he was at the gym by six. Collecting his brand-new card he went in to find Meg. She smiled, her slightly lopsided smile. 'Your friend not here then?'

'He must be on his way.' Chamath looked at his watch. 'Should be here any minute.'

'He's gorgeous, isn't he?' she said dreamily. 'A really beautiful man. Shame about the divorce.'

'*Divorce?*'

'Yeah. Says he can't *look* at another woman right now. Put him right off relationships, it has.' She laughed. 'Never mind,' I said. 'I'll wait!'

At this point Stelios came in. 'You giving away all my secrets, doll?'

They trained together for a while in silence.

'How about a drink afterwards?' Meg said.

'Don't think so, doll.' He patted Chamath's head. 'It's way past this young fella's bedtime.'

They finished early and said goodbye to Meg.

Walking up the High Street with Chamath, Stelios said: 'She fancies you, you know. I can tell.'

'Yeah? I thought it's you she fancies. And why did you tell her you were divorced?'

Stelios looked sheepish. 'To put her off.'

'Funny. If anything, seems to have made her more keen.'

'What?' Stelios grinned. 'You think I'm after *her*? I'm a happily married man. And good to my wife, too.' He stopped in the middle of the street and looked at Chamath. 'I even let her sleep with *you*.'

Shh! Chamath wanted to say, people will hear you.

They began walking again, up to the bus stop on the Common. 'And on that topic, I just want to warn you, son. No monkey business behind my back, understand? She's yours when I say.' He squeezed Chamath's shoulder hard. 'Only when.'

And then—almost because it was a question he had vowed never to ask again—it came out of him unbidden: 'Why am I here?' he asked softly.

Stelios smiled. 'You mean you don't know? She gets a kick out of you, that's why. Keeps her happy. And I'm happy when she's happy.' The Wimbledon bus came and they hopped on. But he must have forgotten what he just said, because he added: 'She's a good woman. She'll do anything I say.'

Funny, Chamath thought, as he settled himself in for the night alone in the sitting room. In the last twenty-four hours they've each warned me off against the other. There's a turf war going on here. I am a small Third World country over which two superpowers are vying for supremacy, each slightly jealous of the other. I am happy for it to be this way. But I must be careful not to play one off against the other, causing war. There was a smile on his face as he closed his eyes. I could be a metaphor for Sri Lanka itself, he thought.

14

Looking back on those weeks: the days endless, rolling, golden like the countryside after harvest; the nights sweet, sticky and fragrant, of a blue so blue it is beyond black, taking you to places of your mind you have never before inhabited. It strikes you later, these weeks are some of the best you will ever have the good fortune to live through.

It should come as no surprise then when they turn suddenly, like a summer storm waiting just behind that hill over there. All your life you have been ruled by the monsters that lurk behind every twist and turn of the maze: monsters that have to be propitiated with good works and loud promises. Happiness has to be paid and accounted for, with bills and receipts, rupees and cents. So why would it be any different now? You always hope for a reprieve: another week, another month. *Please*. Your foolish heart inhabits happiness so thoroughly when it occurs that there is no room for the possibility of woe. This is the only way you are able to survive: within the small square rooms that form the fool's paradise of your contentment.

The work had taken longer than expected. He asked Constance in to have a look the day before the carpets were due to be laid.

'Not bad,' she said, plainly having expected worse. 'I can see a tenant going for this.'

He saw it through other eyes now, a cosy copy of the brownness of Wimbledon, so different from the stark bare spaceship to which he had been strapped before, as he hurtled through the great spaces of the white sky.

'I'll come day after tomorrow to do a measure up, and you can sign then,' she said. 'By the way how is Jamila?'

'I haven't seen much of her lately.'

'Neither have I. How's her case progressing?'

'Case?'

'Never mind,' said Constance. 'I'll see you in two days.'

Case? he thought after she left. She never told me anything about a case?

It was eleven so he went off to the telephone box to call. There was work tonight, at eight o'clock, somewhere in South London, and he took down the address from Mike. He had only just got back inside the house when the bell rang. It was a registered letter in a brown envelope, OHMS. He signed the receipt and opened it and his whole world fell apart.

Dear Mr Pilimatalawa, it began. He knew immediately what it was. He was being given twenty-eight days to leave the country. It was already the beginning of July. The letter had taken five days to get to him. He had till the 26th. He sat down on the carpet, looking up at the white sky outside.

It had been too good to last, he thought bitterly, no one deserves this much happiness. Or could it be that I have done something so wrong, so heinous that this is the only punishment I deserve? He had never been one for bucking the trend, altering the course of fate: yet this was what he *had* done, by becoming a professional, adopting a life that led down twisted unnatural paths; it seemed only logical then that he would end up at this cliff top, where the only way forward was to jump.

He must have spent the whole afternoon seated there, the sunlight turning horizontal, while his various grotesque future lives played themselves out before him: like children play-acting in clothes found in a trunk in the attic, their faces smudged with their mother's make-up. He could continue as a professional, submerged below the grid, living and dying as one of those shadowy individuals of the underworld that exist in any big city: a necessary Platonic counterpart to the Constances who strut and fret their hours upon the stage above. He could go home and marry the Kandyan princess, submerging himself in yet another more esoteric obscurity. The one honourable option, that of doing a regular decent job in this big city seemed to be the only one unavailable to him. He must have dozed off when he heard the front door open downstairs. Almost before he was fully awake, he found himself down there.

'You have to look at this,' he said. 'Please tell me what to do.'

He followed her into her flat, into what was now an alien country of blue roses and yellow zigzags. He noticed something new on the wall—a child's crayon drawing of a woman, stuck to the wall with blue tack. He sank down on her sofa. Kicking off her shoes she sat next to him, reading the letter. She said nothing for quite a while.

'Don't you think,' she said finally, 'that it would be the best thing all round if you went back?'

It was not the response he had been expecting. He remained silent out of shame, and a sense of betrayal.

'Are you really cut out for this life, Chamath? Are you ready to grow up, lead a decent life? Are you even ready to pay your bills on time?'

He realized he couldn't answer a *yes* to any of these questions. Yet he couldn't understand how any of these questions were a necessary adjunct to any life he might lead, decent or otherwise.

'What I want,' he said hotly, 'is to have the freedom to choose what I *really* want.'

'Which is?'

He paused. 'I don't know,' he said finally, ashamed. 'It's just that I'm not ready to choose yet. I need more time.'

She got up and went to the table. She wrote something down on a piece of paper and gave it to him. 'Go and see her,' she said. 'She'll tell you what to do.'

She remained standing, looking down at him. He got wearily to his feet realizing she wasn't prepared to give him, not even in a small way, what he really wanted: the comfort of an embrace, however fleeting.

'This case of yours,' he said. 'What's all that about?'

'You're not the only one with problems,' she said quietly.

But he wasn't really listening. In his mind he was already far away: the selfish animal within had not been fed its daily dose of love, and was already looking elsewhere, nose quivering, for where he might find it; far away at the end of the District Line perhaps.

The old man woke up in the middle of the night to the sounds of a tropical cyclone raging outside, the branches of the mango tree scraping at the window begging to be let in. His bed was soaking with water gushing down the stem of the ceiling fan onto his mattress. He was in the loo peeing when he heard and smelt the sudden sizzle and burn of bacon in a frying pan. There was a crash and the lights went out. Groping his way back he found on the bed, lit by intermittent flashes of lightning, the ball of the fan, its blades still turning lazily.

That could have been me! he thought with a sudden vicious spurt of rage. I might be dead now, cut to pieces by the fan blades, no one to hear my cries in this storm. He cursed his life then, everyone he had ever known, cursed all those facts of his lonely life that had conspired to bring him to this particular point of his existence.

He thought of all those situations of extreme danger he had lived through in the past and survived, noting only after they had passed how close he had been to the edge at the time, marvelling at the throwaway casualness of his attitude, the luck that was like a ball of string he held in his hand endlessly unravelling. Then you get older, you feel how small the ball has become: perhaps your life only ends, he thought, when the string runs out.

You have been asked to come at eight, which is late for a dinner engagement, and the place is out in the sticks, a good twenty minutes from the nearest tube station, past deserted playgrounds and rubbish tips and industrial yards behind chain link fencing; there are bleak criss-cross streets of what look like doll's houses, none of them showing any sign of habitation.

The man who opens the door to you is so huge you wonder how he manages in such a tiny house. And you go in and he locks the door behind you, and the furnishings are somehow in harmony with this quivering mountain of jelly—all frilly curtains and glass knick-knacks and dolls in costume in glass cabinets. By now you're getting quite good at this so you pre-empt him by saying: So, where'll it be tonight, then?

And he's at the sink which is in the far corner of this room which does as sitting room as well as kitchen, and he points with his meaty paws to the packet of frozen fish fingers bleeding on the draining board.

I thought we'd eat in, he says, all cosy like, and see where it leads us from there.

So we're not going out, then? you ask, your heart sinking. Cosy doesn't come cheap, you add. Cosy'll cost you fifty quid extra.

What? For a darkie like you? You must be joking, he says. They didn't tell me it was a darkie they were sending.

And you know that's a lie because you've seen the takeaway menu and it has pictures in it. You decide, you say brightly, your choice.

Thirty's what they said, thirty's what I'm prepared to pay, he says. Should be enough to keep a boatload of you in curry for a month, shouldn't it? You notice he has something in his hand now, something heavy he's moving from one paw to the other—is it a hammer? You don't want to look too closely.

What? Not happy with thirty? he says. He stands there trying to decide what to do, moving that thing from hand to hand, hand to hand. Go on, he says finally, fuck off out of it before I harm you. But the door is locked and you don't know what to do.

He goes and unlocks it. But he's standing right there with that thing in his hands, and you run past him pissing yourself and you know he's behind you, his hot breath on your neck, and you run and run down empty godforsaken roads, past playgrounds and rubbish dumps, past warehouses and industrial sites till finally you stop, your heart pounding bang-bang-bang, and you look round and he's not there, maybe he never was. And you walk right down the middle of that road, under the lonely sodium lights, along white lines broken and comfortless, and you think *My God. My God,* you think. Why have you forsaken me?

It is two hours before you find yourself back in the known world, and when you do, you go back to Hiley Road. It isn't the night for Wimbledon: there is too much inside you now to be cured by mere love or sympathy. You stand under the lukewarm shower a long time trying to wash off the fear and disgust and self-loathing, and the water turns cold, and you only get out when it is really too cold for your body to take it any longer.

You lie on top of the brand-new-second-hand bed in this alien bedroom, and for once in your life you see yourself accurately for what you really are: a travelling salesman just checked into a third-rate hotel, in a fifth-rate part of the city. Go on, you say to yourself. This is the life you chose. *Enjoy*.

15

He was on the floor, underneath the window, listening out for early morning sounds of traffic far away in Worple Road. There was no sound from the other room; Stelios and Elena hadn't got up yet. Any minute now the sun would break through over the roofs of the houses at the back, flooding his space with light and happiness.

Then he woke up and realized where he actually was, and the weight of everything that had happened yesterday sat on his chest like an over-keen wrestler, and he couldn't breathe. You win, he wanted to say. I give up, now let me go. But the weight sat on, constricting his ribcage so his breath came in short silent gasps. He had twenty-two days left. He closed his eyes. I will not get up today, he thought; there is no difference between twenty-two and twenty-one, or even twenty. A death sentence is a death sentence.

He must have dozed off because next thing he knew the doorbell was ringing.

'Carpets, mate. You deaf or something? I've been ringing and ringing these past ten minutes.'

He helped the carpet fitter up with the rolls of carpet, listening to him gabbling on, answering only when he really had to. It was like making small talk at a funeral. I won't be needing all this, he wanted to say. Cancel the order. I'll be gone in three weeks. But he *did* need it. That was the whole point. The flat would carry on its existence regardless, newly tenanted; only he would be gone. He was the only piece of this enormous puzzle that didn't fit. The rogue piece that had somehow worked its way in unplanned. It was time to leave, to let the picture complete itself the way it was meant to be, without him.

Upstairs in the bedroom he noticed a piece of paper on the floor by the bed. '*Sreela Biswas,*' it said. '*Immigration Advisory Services, 68, The Strand, London WC 2.*' It was the paper Jamila had given him. It's hardly worth the trouble, he thought. But maybe I should give it a go.

The old man rang the bell downstairs. His hair was dishevelled, his eyes red-rimmed through lack of sleep. In his hands he held the ball of the fan awkwardly, one blade twisted up in a gratuitous stroke of avant-garde hilarity. He looked like a manic priest who had bolted in the middle of High Mass with the censer. After what seemed the longest time he could see Bar's face peeping at him at low level through the bars of the grill door.

'Oh, it's you,' she said.

'May I come in?'

She looked suspiciously at the fan in his hand. Finally she opened the door.

'Last night,' he said, his voice almost breaking, 'this fell on my bed. I could have been killed.'

'Nothing is as certain as death and taxes,' she said cryptically. 'What did you expect when you decided to muck about with the wiring?'

'The bed is soaking,' he continued. 'The water gushes in every time it rains.'

'Tch, tch, tch,' she shook her head mournfully. 'That flat was in such fine condition when we handed it over to you. *Mint.*'

With almost religious fervour he placed the ball of the fan under the Sacred Heart. 'Treat this as my one month's notice,' he said, his voice low and dangerous. 'I will move sooner if I find something else before the month is up.'

'You must do what you must do,' she replied with finality.

It was only after he left that he realized Ginnie hadn't been there. Perhaps it was a sign: that there must be no room whatsoever for regret.

'*You didn't!*' said Ginnie in horror, when she came back from Keells with the shopping. '*You couldn't!*'

'I could and I did,' said Bar firmly. 'That man has been nothing but trouble since he moved in. 'Think how much we'll have to spend to repair the damage he's caused.'

'But the tax report?' asked Ginnie frantically. 'He can't go now! I haven't been audited yet!'

The sofa must have been dreamt up by a designer on a particularly sleepless night. Upholstered in yellow corduroy it had an organic shape, like a slightly animated custard that had managed to escape its mould. It wobbled knowingly, like a drunk when sober. Whichever way you sat you ended up looking pregnant. Funnily enough, next to Chamath was a woman who actually was pregnant.

'Mrs Oluwole?' said the smart young Asian girl at the desk. 'Ms Biswas will see you now.'

Mrs Oluwole emerged with difficulty from the custard and wobbled off to her consultation. Chamath sat chewing his nails, surreptitiously examining the girl. Effortlessly superior, she had treated him with haughty indifference when he came in. I have a visa, her whole demeanour proclaimed. You don't. And don't you forget it.

Having dispensed with Mrs Oluwole, Ms Biswas came out of the inner office herself to see him. She was dressed all in black—black dress, black boots—somewhat incongruously for high summer. Chamath explained his circumstances while she looked at him through her wide, horizontal glasses, a sort of Asian Nana Mouskouri.

'You've been here since before 1970?'

He nodded.

'Go home,' she said. 'Write out all the details in a letter addressed to your local MP. Take it to him at his next surgery. He will appeal on your behalf.'

'Who is my local MP?' he asked.

'MP? That is for you to find out.' She gave him an exasperated look that reminded him of Jamila. He wondered how they knew each other, what had brought them together. Surely not a visa problem?

'I'm here to advise you,' she was saying, 'not do your work for you. Now are you clear about what you have to do?'

He nodded. She rose to her feet and swept back to her room. Uncertainly, he wobbled out of the sofa and left the office. He looked at the other girl to say thank you and goodbye as he was leaving, but she was engrossed in a magazine, curling a strand of her long hair round and round her index finger.

He got back in time to pay the carpet-fitter. Cash. It gave him great pleasure to get rid of it. He thought of yesterday's joe and shuddered. He had not bothered to call Embassy Services today. Strike one.

Then he sat down and wrote a letter to his father, his first in a long time. It was a courtly letter, full of old-world charm and reticence. 'I visited the Kumarihamy at Grosvenor House,' he wrote. 'I was somewhat disappointed that her daughter wasn't there. The old lady recited a long list of properties that would be given as dowry.' (He wrote this last bit mischievously, knowing how much it would annoy his father.) 'For my part I am not sure that I want to get married yet. I feel I am too young, and have not yet had enough experience of the world.' He put his pen down and smiled. Not enough experience? Ha!

He picked up the pen again. 'In the meantime I have another idea about Hiley Road. Please hear me out before you say no . . .' He went on to outline his scheme for selling, buying and converting houses. It was so detailed, so persuasive he had almost convinced himself by the end of it of the sureness of his scheme. 'Dearest Appachi,' he concluded. 'Please give this your most serious consideration, and I will be eternally grateful to you. Your loving son, Chamath.'

Nowhere did he mention that he was about to be deported in three weeks. He hadn't processed the information himself. He wasn't ready to propound its implications to anyone else, least of all the stranger in the train compartment that was his father. Besides, his father would have overreacted and ordered him home straightaway. He was very traditional and Kandyan in this respect, and not one for controversies or appeals: If they don't want me, I want them even less, he would have said haughtily. I will simply leave.

Elena found him slumped on the floor in a corner of the sitting room when she got back. 'You look terrible,' she said. 'What happened?'

'I'm being deported,' he replied miserably.

She sank down next to him and held his hand, and her softness enveloped him, the faint perfume of her hair, the powdery notes of her make-up, the subtle natural fragrance of her skin. How can I leave all this? he thought with despair.

'You must fight this,' she said, showing unexpected reserves of steel. 'There must be a way.'

He told her about the advice he had got, the letter to the MP.

'If you need it typed up I can take it in to office,' she offered.

Stelios's reaction was completely different. 'Fuck me, they're going to get you anyhow, mate. Just disappear. They'll never find you. I'll show you how.'

'That's what *he* was going to do,' Elena said fondly, 'before he found me. He owes it all to me. But do I ever get thanked for it?'

Stelios grinned and put his arm around her. 'You get your reward every night, doll.' He pointed at Chamath. 'He's your reward.'

She broke away from his grasp. 'Anyway, you're not out of the woods yourself, remember. Your citizenship's not through yet. I can have you sent back at the flick of my hand.'

He seized her hand as she said this and began covering it with kisses. 'Pleease, Miss. I'm *so* frightened. I'll do anything you say. Promise, Miss, I promise!'

And so, as quickly as that, his troubles were forgotten. They were not going to go away: so why bother dwelling on them?

The old man looked up from the typewriter. If only we had the gift of fast-forwarding time, he thought. How many of those things that meant so much then would be reduced to insignificance now. And conversely, how many things that might have meant so *little* then, would be found later to have had the most profound influence on your life!

His reverie was interrupted by a gentle tap on the door.

'Come in,' he said wondering who it could be, because it wasn't Sakuntala's day. The door opened and his heart gave an involuntary lurch when he saw the angular features, the frizzy hair in the dappled half-light coming through the mango tree.

'I heard what happened,' Ginnie said. 'I am truly, truly sorry.'

The old man looked down, clearing his throat. There was nothing to say. He had moved the bed to a drier corner of the room. He had taped up the loose fan wires with insulation tape and turned the trip switch back on.

'I've asked an electrician, but he can't come till August, and I'll be gone by then. I'll give you his number if you want.'

'Please don't go,' she said. '*Please.*' She kept glancing through the window. 'We'll get the fan fixed, and the leak.'

'That's not the problem,' he said, 'it's the general attitude—'

'My sister will be back in a minute, I have to go,' she interrupted. She seized his hand in both hers. 'Promise me you won't go. Promise?'

He cleared his throat again, saying nothing.

16

Chamath helped Constance with the tape measure. 'We want the longest length internally,' she explained. 'So we measure not to the chimney breast but into one of the alcoves either side. Gives you an extra nine inches.' She winked. 'Not that you need it, I'm sure.'

He couldn't believe this was the same girl who had snubbed him so graciously that first day. She's being so nice now, he thought, but I am no different to what I was three weeks ago. The only thing that's changed is the flat. And it did look amazing, the carpet somehow blanking out the mediocre paintwork. In the language of the city you are judged by what you possess, he told himself, those totems that give you power and significance. Your jeans may have holes in them but your flat has carpets. Henceforth you are the carpet man. He thought with slight regret of his previous carpetless life. There was no going back now.

Constance beamed at him. 'Please don't take this personally,' she said laying a perfectly French-manicured hand on his arm. 'It would be good if you weren't around when I showed the place to clients. Perhaps you could take the last of your stuff downstairs, get it out of the way?'

'Downstairs?' he asked, puzzled.

'Oh, I thought . . .?' She put a hand to her mouth. 'Silly me, forget I said that. Wherever it is you're moving to when you let this flat—perhaps you could move there now?'

'Oh Norton,' said Gary. 'Mr Posh. Do you play tennis? How d'you like to go to Wimbledon?'

He almost replied, I don't have to go there, I already live there.

'It's for Friday, all day, 9.30 to 5.30. She'll pay you for two sessions. You do the maths.'

'Is it suit and tie?'

Gary laughed. 'Bollocks to that! You must never look as if you're trying too hard. Jacket and open-necked shirt. You have a jacket?'

He thought of his school blazer with the brass buttons. Gary gave him an address in St John's Wood and rang off.

From the telephone box he walked down to the

corner shop. He looked up as he passed the flat. Soon it would have no connection to him whatsoever; it would merely be a statistic on a piece of paper. He would have all the kudos of ownership, with none of the powers of possession. He would be like any other fat city cat, booted up but emasculated. And that made him sad.

If he was truly honest with himself, power was one of the reasons he liked his work as a professional so much. He had come to realize that often, sex was the least important part of a client's requirements. What they really wanted was for you to possess their soul, take responsibility for their actions and inactions, justify their excesses, condone their weaknesses. To be good at the job you had to offer so much more than mere inches: you had to offer the all-expenses-paid comfort, the eat-all-you-want buffet of your own soul. You had to throw open your arms and say, *For these few hours I will be responsible for all the good and bad in your world, the rights and the wrongs. Leave it with me, don't worry your pretty little head over it*. You were there to give them absolution. In return they gave you money, the notes creased and shop-soiled; and guilt-edged.

He stopped to say hello to the young couple at the organic shop. She was heavily pregnant, resembling one of the papayas in her window. Then he went into the corner shop next door.

'Mr Shafeeq, who is our local MP?' he asked.

'John Baron,' said Mr Shafeeq, 'Labour MP for Brent. Grumpy old geezer.'

'You've had dealings with him?'

'I worked for him this last election.'

'Does he have something called a surgery?'

Mr Shafeeq smiled. 'Funny term, isn't it? When I first heard it I thought it was a free government clinic, or something they had for poor people, like they used to in Kampala. He sees people every Thursday morning at his office on Willesden High Road.'

'Are there huge crowds of people to see him?'

'What do you think?' said Mr Shafeeq.

Chamath bought a biro and a pad of foolscap paper from him and went round the corner to the library. Sitting down at a table he began to set down the sad facts, the sordid details of his life so far.

'You never told us you were at Oxford?' Elena said, looking at the draft.

'It's not something I like to advertise.' He laughed. 'I live in dread that one of these evenings I'll be hired by someone who'll recognize me from back then.'

'What would you do?'

Chamath shrugged. 'Money is money. If there's going to be blame and shame, shouldn't it fall equally on both sides?' He paused. 'At least that's the theory. I know in practice it doesn't work like that.'

He thought: there were those against whom the odds were stacked from birth; they always got the blame. 'And you,' he asked hesitantly. 'Do *you* blame me?'

'Blame you for what?'

'For doing what I do.'

'Why should we? We were the ones who hired you. You only became our friend *afterwards*.'

'But doesn't it bother you that I still go out to work, see other people?'

She laid a hand on him tenderly. 'It's not as if we own you, Chamath—'

'Don't we?' Stelios interrupted. '*I* thought we owned this young bloke.' He grinned at Chamath.

Elena turned to her husband. 'He's been to Oxford,' she said. 'Did *you* even get as far as your O levels?'

'No, doll, I didn't. Come to think of it I didn't get as far as my oats this morning either.' He began to nuzzle the back of her neck, looking at Chamath and winking. Distractedly she pushed him away. Finishing the letter she folded it and put it away in her handbag.

That night Stelios roasted a leg of lamb pumped full of whole cloves of garlic. He deep-fried a panful of potatoes, drained them of the oil and shook some Greek herb into them. A generous splash of sweet sherry and he closed the lid to let them steam gently for five minutes. He brought it to the table and opened the lid.

'Close your eyes and breathe in,' he said. 'We're eating in Cyprus tonight.'

They were a good way beyond drunk now, and after dinner he allowed himself to be led into the bedroom. But halfway through, a disturbing thought occurred to him. Is this a mercy fuck? Have they taken pity on me? Am I being treated to a mercy fuck here? But like the meal it was too delicious to be turned down. And he was too far in, in the most indelicate sense of the word, to pull out now. Besides, he didn't want to seem like an ungrateful bastard, did he? I'll suffer through it, he thought grimly. *Oh Lord, just see how I suffer!*

After all, it had been an easy decision to change his mind and stay: just the fact of Ginnie coming up the stairs on her own had been enough. But one little thing worried the old man. Had she done it out of pity? If that's the case, I'll leave now, he thought. I can stand anything but pity. But even as he postured this way and that, in his mind he knew he had invested too much in this game plan, gone too far, to let it go so easily.

Today, much against his will—more in the spirit of knowing thine enemy—he had promised to visit the Beast in his lair.

'Come for coffee!' the Beast had said. 'I've got Puerto Rican. And,' he winked to show the special significance of this, 'I've got *Doritos*!' He waited for the exclamations of surprise and gratitude that never came, so he continued. 'Yes, I knew that would make your day! Oh, yes *sir*!'

The old man refrained from asking what a Dorito was. He would find out soon enough.

The lift wasn't working. The old man trudged up to the third floor clutching a tin of peaches, the only thing he could find among his possessions worthy of being presented as a gift.

'Come in, brother!' said the Beast. From behind him the actual beast, the harlequin Great Dane, leapt on the old man nearly knocking him down. 'Tiny!' said the Beast. 'Down boy, down! He just *lurves* company, as do I.'

Don, thought the old man. I must remember to call him Don. As in Done. Done and Dusted. Ought to be Done away with. There was a very real danger he would open his mouth and call him 'Beast' to his face.

The Beast—sorry, Don!—took the proffered brown paper bag with circumspection. 'Peaches,' he said. 'Hm, interesting.' He insisted on showing the old man around his flat. (Why do people force you to do this? the old man thought petulantly. I have no interest in seeing how other people live!)

'You can see I have all mod cons,' said Don. 'I have a dishwasher. But I don't cook much. I'm careful about what I eat. I weigh my food. That's the only way I can be *exactly* sure how much goes in.'

The old man refrained from asking whether he weighed what came out, to be *exactly* sure. Instead he said, 'I have a dishwasher too. She comes in once a week.'

There was a second, then a loud guffaw. 'You're priceless!' Don said. 'Priceless!'

From the sitting room balcony there was a view of Marine Drive and the sea.

'Every time I see the little lady in her red tracksuit we make a dash down there, don't we, Tiny? She likes me, I can tell. Of course her smaller sister does her best to prevent us from talking.' He sighed. 'Star-crossed lovers, that's what we are.'

The old man had much the same opinion of Bar, especially after that last episode with the ceiling fan. But hearing her criticized in public like this by an outsider brought out a certain proprietary loyalty in him. 'I think you'll find that the smaller one, Bar, has a heart of gold. I also personally think,' said the old man cunningly, 'that she has extraordinarily fine features.'

'Does she? My goodness, I never noticed. I don't think I've looked at her that closely.'

The old man observed that two doors down, between them and the sea, there was a building site. He noticed the one-inch tor steel bars in the construction. Five storeys, he thought, maybe six. In three months time, Don's view would be gone. But he wasn't about to become the purveyor of bad tidings.

From the kitchen Don produced with a flourish a bowl of Doritos. With suitable exclamations of gratitude the old man set upon it. He had always been a sucker for fast food. Artificial sliced ham, sliced white bread, white sugar. White women.

Don himself didn't eat anything. 'I noticed you admiring my forearms,' he said. 'No, don't deny it. Did you know I was third runner-up in the Mr Antioch pageant two years running? Here, let me show you the pictures.'

'Nooo,' the old man wanted to howl. 'Noo!' Too late. Don produced an album kept conveniently close to the Doritos. There were lots of pictures of a much younger Don with a great big mop of hair, prancing around flexing his biceps.

'You notice I had hair then? I can't wait to show these to the little lady.'

'Who? Bar?' the old man asked innocently.

'Her too,' Don conceded.

The old man had a great desire to lecture this huge gullible American about the dangers of adding up the sum total of his past lives and dwelling upon them. But then he thought of his own manuscript. Was that not a summing up too, just as much as the photo album? And who was going to read and dwell upon it if not himself?

The sisters had observed the old man going across the road. It was unusual enough to find the old man stepping out of his annexe in the morning. To be seen going across the road with a brown paper bag was nothing short of outrageous.

'He's going to see Don,' said Ginnie.

'He's going to see *what* done?'

'You know. The beast. His name is Don.'

'Dun? What an appalling name for a mother to give a child. Why would He be going to see *him*?'

'I don't know,' said Ginnie. 'Maybe they're planning something. Maybe they're planning to enter our house in the dead of night and ravish us in our beds.'

'Ginnie, really! Your mind is like a sewer sometimes.'

'I live in hope,' Ginnie said sadly. 'Somehow that hope is never realized.'

An hour later they saw the old man returning minus the paper bag.

'Men,' said Bar. '*Men!*'

17

John Baron, MP, sat inside a glass cubicle within a small office on the Willesden High Road, overflowing with East Africans, West Africans, South Asians and East Europeans. Chamath took a number and awaited his turn, sweltering in his school suit and school prefect's tie.

Through the wide window glass he watched the street life outside, traffic wardens and old-age pensioners, young mothers with heavy shopping and tramps: all those lucky people who were not about to be deported. Any minute now he expected Jonas to walk past; but he didn't.

The MP was middle-aged with longish hair, thinning on top but curling over a lavishly dandruffed collar. He wore glasses and a hearing aid, so every other sentence was punctuated with a *What? What was that? What did you say?* or a *Speak up, I can't hear you!* This made life outside the cubicle rather exciting. You were able to absorb in the greatest detail the secret crises of other people's lives. Through the rather long morning he learnt about genital mutilation in Hargeisa, honour killing in Kampala and the unreasonable inflation this year of the bride price in Kano. When it came to his turn his own tale was sadly tame.

'Oxford,' said John Baron. 'Hmm.'

Chamath sat there nervously while he read the letter.

'And school?'

'I was at boarding school,' Chamath shouted. 'I came here in 1968.'

'All right, all right, you don't have to shout,' said John Baron good-naturedly.

It really was a banal story. No mutilations, no murder. The immigrants swiftly lost interest, going back to their daily business of clicking prayer beads and reading holy books; suckling children and nibbling surreptitious chapattis from Tupperware boxes.

'I'll put this up to the Home Office,' John Baron said finally.

'Thank you,' Chamath shouted.

'It's important to remember that while your appeal is being heard you are not allowed to work.' He looked hard at Chamath. 'Absolutely no work. Understand?'

Outside, it must have been the hottest day of the year; he longed for a swim. Then he thought of Jamila. He had not seen her for more than a fortnight. This appeal— whether successful or not—had been directly due to her. He owed her a report. The least he could do was to tell her what had happened. She wasn't at home. Unwilling to sit in the flat, he changed out of his suit and went to the library. Lately this had been his refuge, his second home. He had begun to recognize many of the old men who came there every day, pretending to read the newspapers on their long sticks simply because they had nowhere else to go, nothing else to do with their time. (It had taken him a while to realize that many of them didn't even bother to turn the pages, sitting motionless in their shabby overcoats, eyes closed as if in prayer.)

Sitting down, he realized how little he actually knew Jamila. They had met when he first moved in, and fallen into that easy pattern of some-days-sex, some-days-not.

'Sex to a man is like a hot meal,' she had said once. 'It means absolutely nothing.'

'And to a woman?' he asked cheekily. 'It means the whole world, right?'

'Don't flatter yourself,' she said slowly. 'In some things I'm more man than you.'

She had been born in Port-of-Spain, Trinidad, her family arriving in London when she was only two. She went back to Trinidad once every five years or so. 'It's like a village,' she said. 'They don't forget who you are. They like to keep up with what you're doing, who you're with, how many children you have.'

'I know,' he said. 'It's the same at home. So how do you cope?'

'I lie,' she said. 'I lie through my teeth. The worst is they know I'm lying but there's no way they can prove it. They'd get the truth out of my parents in a second. Luckily for me they're too old to travel!'

Unlike him she had made the quantum leap into this other civilization, learning its language, becoming adept in its dark arts. He envied her this fluency, this expertise, because he was beginning to realize it was something he would never achieve: he would always be the foreigner at the table, the one who never quite got it right, the one who never knew which fork to use. The one they were all waiting to talk about the moment he left the room.

So why then did he so desperately want to stay? I don't like my choices taken away from me, he thought. I want the luxury of being able to say no without having it said for me. I am the child in the ice cream shop who doesn't want to choose his three flavours because the moment he does, he has limited himself to those three and can't have anything else. Far better to be suspended as long as possible in that glorious moment when everything's a possibility, even if at the same time nothing's a possibility.

He felt a tap on his shoulder. Looking up, he saw Jamila.

'You!' he said beaming. 'I've just been thinking about you.'

'You haven't been around these last few weeks,' she said.

'I went to the Immigration Advisory Service. Met your friend Sreela. To cut a long story short, our local MP is appealing on my behalf. Isn't it fantastic?'

One of the old men at the table glared at him. 'Shh!' he said. 'Can't you see we're trying to do some work around here?'

'Let's go outside,' she whispered, giggling.

Outside, the sun had left the sky but the light remained, like a slow-fading memory of a better time.

'Come back to the flat,' she said. 'I need your advice on something.'

It was already past his gym time. They would be expecting him in Wimbledon, anxious to know how this important day in his life had gone. He hesitated. 'I'm really sorry,' he said reluctantly. 'They'll be waiting for me at home.'

'They?' she said, her eyes narrowing. '*Home?*'

He shook his head. 'It would take too long to explain.'

'Chamath what's going on? Two months ago you were a decent regular guy. How could you sink into the gutter so quickly?'

He got angry. 'If that's the way you feel I can't help it,' he said. 'And they're *not* people from the gutter.'

'Yeah, right. I saw the girl that morning. Oh, Chamath, Chamath,' she said despairingly. 'We try so hard to be respectable, do the decent thing, because we know damn well the whole lot of us are on the line here.' There were tears in her eyes now. 'All it takes is one bad apple. For *all* of us to be judged by your rotten standards.'

He turned and began walking away, into the blue twilight, darkening imperceptibly now. Those tears, he thought. They're not only for the immigrant community I seem to have let down so badly. There's more to it than that.

You're in your sixth form blazer with the brass buttons on it and an open-necked polo shirt, and you're going up the lift in a grim St John's Wood purpose-built apartment block. The door is opened by your josephine, a harassed-looking older woman (not old, actually, though not young) who has one of the most charming smiles you have ever seen when she smiles, which is not often, a smile that goes right into her eyes and drenches them with light. Eyes you could drown in. And in the corner—well, what do you know?—there's this grim hatchet-faced kid; and the mother catches you looking at her.

Oh, she's not interested in tennis, the mother says,

she would die rather than go to the tennis with me, she's always been like that, she says.

There is almost nothing in this enormous flat, all bleached and grey, bleak and blank, but its very emptiness stinks to you of riches, because by now you have developed a fine nose for these things; you can sniff out the bouquet, the aura of a rich josephine at fifty yards, like a pig with a truffle. And the only warmth in this endless wasteland of accommodation comes from one baroque splash of colour on the end wall, a gigantic oil painting both brazen and licentious, and far too big for this low-ceilinged room. From our country house in Scotland, she says, from the days when we had a country house. My husband's grandfather had mills up there.

He's the one who bought the debenture seats, she says, negotiating the heavy traffic into Wimbledon in a beat-up blue station wagon (Oh, how deep the rich bury their truffles!).

And you have no idea what debenture seats are, except that you're sitting in one, the best that money can buy too, right at the net on Centre Court.

When they were building Wimbledon, she says, they didn't have enough money so they passed the hat round, and anyone who subscribed was given seats in return. Did you know that they're bought and sold on the Stock Exchange now? And you've never heard of chairs being bought and sold like that, but there you go, that's life in the big city for you.

And then my husband goes and dies on me, she says, leaving me with Tess, who's not at all cheap to educate as you can imagine. So this is my last week.

Last week? you say in alarm. For the seats, she says patiently, as if explaining things to a dumb-fuck, which is essentially what you are. I'm selling them once the finals are over.

And it's Roscoe Tanner on Centre Court now, the man with the fastest serve in the universe, and all you see is the flash of his metal racket in the sun, and the ball is gone, and the crowd goes *aah!* as if he's sprinkled holy water all over them. And there's the Duke of Kent up there in the royal box and everyone has to curtsy to him, and can you see who's two rows back? she asks, but don't look now, don't make it too obvious. And you half expect it to be Princess Michael again in a very large white hat, but no, it's only (*only!*) Julie Andrews. They come every year, your josephine says, she and her mother, they own those two seats.

And on your way to lunch you pause awhile at Court no. 1 where Betty Stove is hammering away at Martina Navratilova, the two of them going at it like mastodons at play. And upstairs, in the holy of holies, she buys you a smoked salmon sandwich and a gin and tonic. That's what we call the plebs lawn, she says, pointing through the window to the grass below. I just wanted to enjoy all of this one last time, she says, and I wanted a good-looking man to enjoy it with. And she sighs because it occurs to her that next year, if she comes at all, she'll be down there herself with all those plebs.

And you get back to watch Evonne Goolagong against Chris Evert in the afternoon and when that's over she says shyly, I know it's after your time but would you like a little early supper? And because it's food and you never say no to food, and just maybe because of that smile, but mostly because you're the dumb-fuck that you are, you say yes. So you give the day's passes to the hungry people standing in line outside and you go back to St John's Wood and the hatchet-faced kid, and you eat the roast lamb and mint sauce in the oppressive silence of this concrete flat, and it's nothing like the lamb you had in Cyprus last night because that was cooked with love. And when you leave she says, thank you, you made one of my last days really special, and hatchet-face glares at you because she is the self-appointed guardian of her mother's morals—*oh yes*, she knows what's been going on here, what this is all about!—and you realize that if not for her you might actually have stayed on against your better judgment because really, you're getting weaker and dumber as time goes on.

And you leave with the sixty quid safely in your pocket and she's closed the door on you even before you've got to the lift, and in the loneliness of that long concrete corridor you think, rather wistfully: Who's she going to take tomorrow to the finals? *Why didn't she ask me?*

Next morning there was a letter from his father on the mat. He took it upstairs.

Dear Chamath,

I received your letter today, and I don't quite know what to say. We got the mortgage on that flat with the greatest difficulty while you were still up at Oxford, only by proving that I was able to send money on a regular basis to fund your (rather high!) fees. It occurs to me that if we now sell the flat, that particular mortgage will cease to exist. You will then have to apply for a new one, without the benefit of a track record. Do you have regular employment? Can you show a regular amount of money going into the bank every month for them to establish your earning capacity? I thought not. In the unlikely event that you were able to get a mortgage for a future purchase, I would unhesitatingly give you permission to sell. Till then you will have to sit tight, I am afraid.

I met Elsie last week. I do wish you wouldn't wilfully give other people the wrong impression. She is under the misapprehension that you are an amazingly successful and dynamic young man, going round collecting rents on my behalf. I did my best to convince her that there was only one property, and as yet no rent. She naturally prefers to believe your version as it is more glamorous.

Dear boy, please look after yourself. You cannot imagine how much I miss you.

Your loving

Appachi

Well, you won't have to wait long if this appeal fails, Chamath thought, putting the letter away. In three weeks from now I'll be knocking at your door. It seemed to him that at last his life was being given back to him stripped of choice; he was coming into possession of its lean and emaciated body. He looked at his surroundings through the restricted vision, the narrowed eyes of a man who has already left them: they had ceased to have any meaning. His mind quite simply refused to record its sensations and sentiments because it foresaw their irrelevance; like a doctor who has washed his hands off a terminal patient.

He went off to the Willesden pool and spent the next hour swimming lengths in mindless oblivion, vaguely

aware through the blue-green glass of the blue-green
life outside. Afterwards he ambled up the High Road.
Walking behind a young couple pushing a child in a
buggy, he suddenly became aware of who it was.

'Jonas,' he said softly. Jonas turned round. The girl
who was with him walked on, pushing the stroller.

'My man,' Jonas said, clapping him on the back.
'What's up?'

'How many times I've walked around here hoping
to bump into you,' Chamath said happily.

'Are you still working for . . .?'

'Yes,' said Jonas quickly. 'And you?'

Chamath nodded. He looked towards the girl with
the pushchair, but she was out of earshot, waiting
patiently a few yards away. He noticed she was Asian.
'I didn't know you had a family. I mean I thought . . .'

'Thought what?' Jonas said a little aggressively.
'What are you trying to insinuate?'

But Chamath wasn't about to be drawn into argument
with someone he genuinely felt affection for. 'How do
you manage the nights?' he asked. 'Does she know?'

'You crazy? I told her I'm on shift work. Night
watchman in a warehouse, that's what I am!'

They both looked at this Asian girl, so young you
couldn't believe she already had a child of her own, a
child of two or three. Jonas's voice softened. 'They're
all I have, man. I'll do anything to give them a roof over
their head. Understand?'

Chamath was silent. After a while he said softly, 'There's this new disease they're talking about. Be careful. Please.'

'Don't I know it,' Jonas said quietly. 'Don't I know it.'

'So, shall we meet up one of these days?' Chamath asked hopefully. 'Have a drink?'

Jonas shook his head. 'No, man. My life's way too complicated. You know what I mean?' He embraced him silently, with a pressure so strong it belied the sentiment of his words. Then he was gone.

Chamath watched the three of them as they disappeared up the High Road, and he prayed to the God he didn't believe in: that they would always be together, in the one country; that they would always remain in good health. It was only afterwards it struck him that he hadn't said anything about his own troubles: for those brief few minutes they had receded to where they properly belonged in the greater scheme of things: a small poisonous shrub, glossy and flourishing, in the endless tropical jungle of other people's woes.

18

It was a day like any other at Bubbles. The ceaseless grind of the Bambalapitiya traffic hardly penetrated the gloom of the little cottage, shielded as it was from the road by the junk-filled garage and the old man's annexe above. The ladies were late risers who didn't believe in breakfast.

'Just a cup of Harischandra coffee for me, dear. Black, two sugars.'

'I'll have mine white, one sugar.'

'What do you mean *white, one sugar*? Get up and go make your own. And while you're at it make one for me!'

And so they squabbled on gently, in adjoining beds, each trying vainly to outlast the other because the rules of the game were that whoever got up first made the coffee. Generally it was way past noon when someone, usually Ginnie, capitulated. And by then it was time for lunch.

Lunch was easy. They got themselves two takeaway packets from *The Banana Leaf* three blocks away. On this they could never agree, whether they wanted a fish lunch, or chicken or vegetarian. The only way was for them both to go. Even then it was a constant source of irritation.

'I think I win today, dear. There's *much* more chicken in mine than there's fish in yours.'

'I'm so glad, dear. You need the protein, eat up.'

'What do you mean, *you need the protein, eat up?*'

'Legs, dear. Your legs.'

'What's wrong with my legs?'

'Well, Daddy always thought they were— you know, how can I put this nicely?—a leetle rickety?'

In all matters of opinion and taste Daddy's word was final. It didn't matter in the slightest that he had been dead these last twenty years.

That morning they had got up unreasonably early— at eleven—and were now in that dead hour before lunch, Ginnie listlessly leafing through back copies of *HI!!* magazine, and Bar reading the *Old Joe's* newsletter. Daddy had attended St Joseph's; even two decades after his passing, the newsletter appeared promptly every month on the door mat.

'Oh, look! The Josephian Carnival is on this week.'

'Do you remember The Sweet Shop?'

'*Do I remember The Sweet Shop!*'

For three glorious years—Daddy had been alive

then—Bar and Gin had run the sweet shop at the Joe's Carnival, making the most money of any stall. Every day there had been a different cake to raffle, milk toffees, love cake, kalu dodol and easily twenty other varieties of sweets.

'Do you remember the merry-go-round, do you remember the bumper cars?'

'Do you remember the boys?'

'You *would* remember the boys, wouldn't you.'

'I was only just saying . . .'

'I know,' said Bar springing up. 'Let's go!'

'Are you crazy? You forget you're almost sixty-five!'

'Well, we could ask Him to take us.'

'*Him?* That's rich! I thought you were the one who said, "Please let him go, I can't handle gold-digging tax inspectors sniffing around Daddy's millions."'

'Well . . .'

'You just want to get on the dodgems.'

'So what if I do?'

As it happened, the old man refused point blank. 'Carnivals?' He shook his head and a look of extreme pain flickered across his face. 'I don't do carnivals. Sorry.'

So they went with Don who was only too willing. Ginnie wore the beige pant-suit she'd had run up by Apothecary's Tailors in 1976. ('It still fits, so why shouldn't I wear it?') Bar wore a flowery mini circa 1969. For added dash she topped it off with a red beret.

'A mini? Are you sure dear? With those legs?'

'Let's not start all that again, dear. If you carry on like this you'll end up giving me a complex.'

The Sweet Shop was a thing of the past now, but the rides had got more wicked in the intervening years. Also more expensive. The grounds of St Joseph's were filled with young revellers.

'Ah, this!' said Don. 'This is what I came back for! A *wunnerful* slice of Surrey Lankan culture!'

Bar headed straight for the bumper cars, Don squeezing in by her side with difficulty.

'Whee!' said Bar flying past, crashing through. Don had experienced the worst parts of drug-ridden Oakland, drive-by shootings and freeway pile-ups. Nothing had prepared him for this.

Two students elbowed past Ginnie who was watching this spectacle of her sister making a grown man cry. (It was not the first time.)

'Excuse me, Achie!' they said, pushing through.

'Don't you *Achie* me,' she wanted to reply. 'I'm still in my prime. See that man in the bumper car there? You realize he's after me?' She thought of Him back home. *And there may be others too, though I'm not sure: I'm still working on it.*

When they got back home it was almost midnight but the old man's light was on, his curtains drawn in blood-red protest. Ginnie was all for inviting Don in for a hot cup of Milo but Bar wouldn't hear of it. So she kissed him good night on the doorstep. 'Thanks for a *wunnerful*, I mean wonderful, night,' she said.

The appeal might take months, and Chamath floated in this limbo of indecision. Some days he didn't bother calling Embassy Services; but by next day guilt had kicked in and he was promptly at the phone by eleven. A professional with a conscience? Bet that's a novelty in this trade, he thought.

In the mornings he swam. In the afternoons he trained. It pleased him to look lean and buff. It didn't hurt his night-time career either. Both he and Meg tended to arrive at the gym at the same time, a little before Stelios who—predictably perhaps—formed their favourite topic. The worst thing about someone else's lying was that *you* had to lie too in order to protect them. He was very careful never to mention Elena. According to Meg Stelios led a sad and solitary existence, a tragic hero battling the odds this world had stacked against him. Chamath tried hard not to laugh. How much of this Stelios had told her and how much she had imagined was hard to tell. Chamath's job was to corroborate not contradict.

It was only years later that it struck him: How

reasonable we were back then! How laid back we were about other people's sins! Perhaps the true hallmark of old age was not fading looks or defective memory, but intransigence.

'You know he's taking me to the Notting Hill Carnival?' she said excitedly. 'You want to come?'

'I may not be around by then.'

'Oh, yes, I forgot. You might have been deported!' She chuckled.

He thought: Gee, thanks, Stelios. I religiously protect your story, your fine fabric of lies. You tell mine to the whole world. But he wasn't angry. In spite of everything he worshipped his friend. Old truths died hard: in his dealings with them he was still the rescue dog; he would always be so.

That evening Stelios said: 'Let's all go on holiday. I think we deserve to treat ourselves.'

They saw the look on his face. 'We'll pay for you,' they said. 'You be our guest. Seriously.'

'I wouldn't hear of it,' he replied. 'I have money. But my visa? I'm stuck here till they take a decision.'

'Oh, you'll get it. It's only a matter of time.'

Stelios grinned. 'You remember Ibiza last year? The nudist beach? Let's go there.'

Then the words came out of his mouth, unplanned. 'Sri Lanka,' he said. 'Why don't we go to Sri Lanka?'

Suddenly it seemed that this was the only option there had ever been. Why hadn't they thought of it before? The idea took hold of them, setting their minds ablaze, crackling with every recondite and exotic possibility.

But later, when he was alone in his nest of sheets on the floor, he thought: Is this wise? He well knew the element of fantasy there was, of play-acting, when your life was transposed to another country. It was this fantasy that fuelled the dreams of so many immigrants, as much as economics or the promise of political freedom. And his own English dream was no different. But going back to Sri Lanka even temporarily would mean reverting to reality. How would his friends fare in the harsh light of that tropical truth? Will I think any less of them in that setting? He feared for them the way a Sri Lankan man fears for his foreign bride when he takes her home the very first time.

He argued with himself: The only opinion that stands to change is your own. Are you telling me you're not in control of it? But he knew only too well the answer to that one. Even as a professional it had always been the image he sold, the sexual *frisson* more than the sex itself. Once the image was gone, once your true colours were exposed to someone else, they could not later unlearn that truth. Hadn't that been his fear that day when Elena saw him in the surroundings of his grim flat?

At Hiley Road there was a note from Constance, 'Please ring. Urgent.'

'I think I have a tenant for you,' she said when he rang. 'He's coming in today to pay a deposit, and we'll be checking on his references. You can come in to sign the contract when it's ready. In the meantime do you have a contact number and address?'

He hesitated. Then he gave the Wimbledon details. It was an imposition, but there was no alternative he could think of. They won't mind, he thought. More than ever he felt bound to them now.

That afternoon he came back early and measured the kitchen. He had an idea. The only worthwhile thing I have to offer them is the use of my builder's hands, he thought. Their kitchen needs tiling. They had stretched their budget to buy this flat, and in this expensive location too. He worked out he would need 110 feet of tiles and two eight by four sheets of one-inch plywood.

'I'm taking you to B&Q this weekend,' he said. 'Choose your tiles. I'm going to do up your kitchen for you.'

He could see they were pleased but puzzled. 'We invited you to stay because we wanted you here,' she said. 'You don't have to feel you need to repay us in any way.'

'You don't understand, I *want* to do this,' he replied. 'It gives me the greatest pleasure in the world.' It was true: he felt supremely happy because in some small way it put him back in charge again.

The whole of Wimbledon seemed to be buying home

supplies that weekend. She chose a plain matt black
tile for the floor and walls, to contrast with the honey-
coloured wooden cupboards. He was thankful because
plain tiles made his job that much easier. They loaded
the tiles into the GTI.

'Let's *carry* the plywood sheets back,' Stelios said.
The car didn't have a roof-rack, so there was in fact
no other way of bringing it home; but it was one of
those mad ideas he would remember the rest of his
life. Stripped to the waist in the August sun, they had
to stop every hundred yards or so for a breather. The
non-stop stream of cars on Worple Road tooted at them,
more than a few women drivers slowing down to make
cheeky comments and blow kisses. It took over an
hour, and they were not much good for anything else
the rest of the day; except to wrap themselves around
two bottles of Rioja.

He began to tell them about Sri Lanka, the two-
thousand-year-old cities, the vast man-made reservoirs
called *tanks*. 'At that time they were the finest hydraulic
engineers in the world,' he said. 'Those tanks still
supply most of what we use for irrigation.' He told them
about Kandy—the last capital of the longest-surviving
continuous monarchy in the world—which fell to the
British in 1815. He told them about his illustrious
ancestor the treasurer, and he smiled because he was
beginning to sound exactly like his mad father.

He told them about the beaches of the east coast and

the Bay of Trincomalee, considered by Napoleon the finest natural harbour in the world. He told them about the ebony and the elephants, the cinnamon and the sapphires, till they were as drunk with dreams as with wine, and outside it was dusk and the sky darkened slowly, slowly, to the blue of those very same sapphires.

It occurred to Chamath that whether he was deported or not, he would be in Sri Lanka shortly. So he wrote to his father.

Dear Appachi,

I have some good news. I'll be coming home soon! Isn't that great? It'll probably be for just a week or so, but you never know, it might be for longer. (I may even decide to stay for good.) I'll be bringing some very good friends of mine—they have been like family to me here, and I owe them a huge debt of gratitude. I know you will like them—they are called Elena and Stelios (she's Spanish and he's Cypriot) and in fact I am staying with them at the moment.

I have taken on board what you said about selling the flat, and I won't be pursuing that idea for the moment. In the meantime, we have a prospective tenant. Please keep your fingers crossed, because we haven't signed up yet!

Your loving son,

Chamath

Just before he sealed the envelope he added the Arterberry Road address at the top, judiciously leaving out the phone number at the flat.

Using a rusty Sandviq saw inherited from the Hippodrome Mews site—how long ago that seemed now!—he set to work on the ply, cutting it to fit the kitchen floor and nailing it down to the joists. He hoped the inch ply was thick enough to withstand the give of the timber. Spreading the adhesive he laid the tiles out, working from the centre to the edges, cutting the strips that fitted under the kitchen units. It was by no means a perfect job but he was grateful to the black because it successfully hid his lack of tiling skills.

That night they got a takeaway because the kitchen was out of bounds. The talk was all of Sri Lanka.

'At long last, a holiday with a bit of culture,' she said, smiling. 'Stelios, how on earth will you manage?'

'Oh, I'm tough, doll. I can take it. Two years with you, I can take anything.'

'I wrote to my father,' Chamath told them.

Next morning he was mixing black cement for the grouting when Constance rang. 'The contract's ready for you to sign. He wants to move in next weekend.'

The stage was set for his exit. The only ties he was now bound by were the ones here at Wimbledon. I am ready to be deported, he said aloud to the empty room. *Come and get me!*

'Norton, Mr Posh, are you up for a job at midnight?'

'What? An all-nighter?'

Mike paused. 'That's what I thought. Actually, no. She wants to take you to a *party* at midnight.'

'What is she? A vampire?'

Mike laughed. 'Don't you go being rude about our clients. You know we only bring you the best!'

Chamath said nothing. He thought of the jelly man with the hammer in his hand, living in the doll's house.

'Norton, are you still there?'

'Yes.'

'So? Are you up to it?'

'Yes,' said Chamath. 'I suppose I am.'

19

It's all right once you're on the job because the adrenalin kicks in, but waiting till midnight without falling asleep is the killer. And wine, sadly, is out of the question for obvious reasons, ha ha. You get to Brixton at a quarter to midnight, to one of those pale pink brick houses at the end of Ferndale Road, and you realize with a shock it's an Indian woman. And why should you be shocked because she's Indian? You don't know, but you just are.

Anyway she's not Indian but Guyanese and her name is Ranjini and she's tiny, in long black leggings and a shirt wrapped round her waist, and the cutest little ring in her nose, the sort of woman who will never have worries about putting on weight. And really, really pretty.

Turns out she works for Lambeth Town Hall in the housing department, assigning flats to the poor, and you think for a moment of Jamila before you banish the thought. And even though she's pretty there's this ineffable look of sadness there, pale violet shadows under those exquisite eyes, and you would like to take that face in your hands and lick the sadness away, every last scrap of it, you can taste the sugar. But you get a grip on yourself. It is only just gone midnight—far too early in the day to be getting sentimental.

'It's them Guyanese,' she says in an accent both lilting and musical, that's neither Guyanese nor Indian but somewhere in between. 'I don't want them looking down their noses at me just because I'm a widow.' She tells you how her in-laws blame her for her husband's premature death, how they have ostracized her for bringing bad luck on the family. A Hindu widow is still today no better than a piece of dead meat picked off a corpse by a crow. I don't want their pity, she says. I picked you because you look Guyanese. I want to give them something to talk about. And you think of Jamila in Port-of-Spain giving *them* something to talk about. Talk seems to be the biggest cash crop of the Third World. If only we could export it!

So she gives you a quick rum (*Mount Gay* of course, crushed lime, brown sugar) and you head off to the other side of Brixton beyond Railton Road, to a large house in a square. And it must be 12.30 by now but they take a long time answering the door and it's the hostess in a blue housecoat, her hair in curlers.

'Ranjini!' she says over-brightly. 'You're early!'

The Professional

So you sit in the sitting room, just the two of you, making desultory small talk on a plush sofa pushed to the far end, while the hostess goes back up to get dressed, shaking her head at how some people, *some people,* don't know their manners, do they? Turning up to parties too early. And finally, the other guests start trickling in an hour or so later and the party gets going.

And it's a strange and wondrous thing, but you've been transported back to the 40s, to the era of Swing bands: and there's Duke Ellington and Bennie Goodman and Artie Shaw; and Billie Holliday, of course, and that god of gods, Louis Armstrong, singing the only song of the evening you recognize, *Mack the Knife*. And your talents are many and varied (as you've been led reliably to understand these last few months) but Swing isn't one of them, which makes your life easier in a way, as you sit on the sofa watching your josephine being swung around by these big black men in shiny suits purple as bruises under the blue neon lights; and the women in their full dresses and lacquered hair who seem to take their dancing more seriously than sex. And there's something deeply formal, almost religious, about these rites and you realize why service has to take place after midnight: these people are expressing themselves in a language unknown to the younger black generations of London, a language that will die out in another twenty years: because you swear there is no one under sixty in that room apart from you and your josephine.

And you leave the party which is still in full swing (ha ha) at four in the morning and she offers to drive you home; or you can stay with me and just sleep, she says with her sad eyes, so you do and of course it's not just sleep is it, it never is, and you leave next morning without the extra fifty which should by rights be in your pocket, and why are you surprised? You're just a dumb fuck aren't you. A dumb fuck who never even learnt to swing properly.

The old man sat looking out at the new leaves on the mango tree. His silent contemplation was shattered by a crash downstairs, a sudden explosion of sound. It took him a full second to realize what it was. Glen Miller's Big Band Sound, playing *In The Mood* to the excited shrieks of the landladies. And then—horror of horrors!—the garden gate opened and Don appeared, in black trousers and black patent leather shoes, and a twinkly purple waistcoat.

He could hear his loud voice at the front door. 'Ladies?' he boomed. 'May I have the pleasure of the first dance?'

The enemy, he thought. The enemy is at the gates.

Chamath very nearly missed the letter. It had been put among others in a pile behind the front door by Jamila; and Chamath had only popped in to clear the last of his stuff before the tenant moved in.

'I have been instructed by the Home Secretary to inform you that your appeal has been upheld . . . Please present this letter, together with your passport, for processing at the Home Office, Lunar House, Wellesley Road, East Croydon.'

And there it was, just like that. He sat on the step trying to take it all in, and he was back once more in that great white blankness of the sky, a speck, all alone. It means nothing, he thought, nothing at all. And that is as it should be. All I wanted was the freedom to be able to choose. Before he left Hiley Road he scribbled on the back of the brown Home Office envelope. *I am in*, he wrote, pushing it under Jamila's door.

'I am allowed to do any job I want,' he explained to them that evening. 'Can you imagine? I don't have to be a professional any more. I can move out and get my own room.'

'Don't be a bloody idiot,' Stelios said sharply. 'You're staying with us. This is where you *belong*.'

Already at 8.45 in the morning there were over fifty people on the pavement waiting for Lunar House to open. It was high summer but a chill wind cut through the canyon formed by the modern concrete buildings on either side of the road. East Croydon: The Eighth Architectural Wonder of the World.

At 9 sharp they were allowed in, up the staircase to the ticket machine. Chamath tried to maintain a dignified pace (he was, after all, a *professional* in a suit) among the stampeding charge of Afghans and Somalis, ending up with ticket number 47, ahead of two heavily pregnant women and a blind man with a cane.

The hall was over a hundred feet in length, plate glass all along one side, and opposite, a row of numbered glass booths. The smoke of yesterday's immigrants still hung heavy in the air (the glass windows could not be opened, so there was nowhere for the smoke to go) and the carpet held the remains of a hundred impromptu picnics. There were rows of benches without backs (Lean back? Just where do you think you are?) and the fifty-odd candidates settled themselves in for the long haul. There were others coming in now, thick and fast, and the ones on the benches looked at them with ineffable superiority. (Even the blind man tapped his cane in a superior manner.)

When his number came up, he presented his passport and letter. Then another couple of hours. By now the place was filled to overflowing and people were sitting on the floor, surreptitiously stubbing out cigarettes on the carpet. There was talk in unintelligible tongues and the wailing of countless babies, many of them—Chamath was sure—being born that very minute. Finally his number was called. The woman behind the glass had curly grey hair and a good-natured smile. She pushed the passport back to him underneath the glass and he saw the pentagonal Home Office seal, signed by 'Mrs Kennedy'.

'I don't know what the fuss was about,' she said. 'You were here well before the 1972 cut-off date. You should have been granted this permanent residency automatically.'

A sudden anger seized him. 'You mean I needn't have spent these last months trawling through the bottom of the pond, eating shit?' he wanted to shout. 'I needn't have sold my soul to the devil to keep alive?' But the anger subsided as quickly as it had risen. There was no space in that enormous hall for his laughably small misfortunes. The sum total of misery in that room was a vast ocean into which his troubles had landed, sailing neatly through the air in an arc, like a gob of spit.

He pocketed the passport with a smile at charming Mrs Kennedy and took the bus home.

20

The morning they were due to fly, a letter from Chamath's father arrived in Wimbledon.

My dear boy,

Was your last letter some sort of joke? Are you about to waste all this money coming home for just a week? I cannot stress enough how inconvenient it is for me that you should be arriving now. For reasons I cannot go into in a letter—you will see well enough when you get here—I will hardly have time to see your friends when they are here.

If your flights are already booked and paid for, which is what I fear, I am afraid your friends will not be able to stay with me. I have spoken to my good friend from childhood, Aelian de Silva, who has a cottage he occasionally lets to tourists if they come with a recommendation. He will reserve it for you. It comes at a very reasonable rate which I am sure your friends will be able to afford. As for you, you know you are always welcome here, even if Poppy and Sita will take a week to clear out the junk which has unaccountably accumulated in your room during your absence.

If, however, you decide to stay with your friends, rest assured dear boy that I shall not take it amiss. I have not seen this cottage of Aelian's—it is in his front garden, and was thrown up rather hastily I understand as dowry for his elder daughter—but even if it is basic, I am sure you will all be very comfortable there.

Since you have not had the courtesy of giving me exact details I will, as the saying goes, see you when I see you. Or rather, I hope and pray you will come to your senses and make this trip at a better time, once you are more established, and when you have given us more time to prepare, so that you and your friends can be received accordingly.

Your affectionate
Appachi

Chamath threw the letter down in despair. He doesn't want to see me! he thought. He certainly doesn't want my friends. It really was the missive of an elderly gentleman on a train, informing you that your proposed occupation of his carriage might be rather inconvenient at the present time. Otherwise, which father would not be glad to see his son, whatever the circumstances?

'What does he say?' Elena asked. Their suitcases were packed and by the front door, awaiting the minicab.

'Oh, he's absolutely delighted. Can't wait to meet you both. We'll call him from the airport as soon as we get in.'

'Call him from here,' she said. 'I thought you'd already done that.'

'No,' he replied quickly. He didn't want to confront his father over the phone. Whatever it was, he would deal with it face-to-face.

But he did have one last call to make, from the public phone in the departure lounge.

'Norton,' said Gary. 'Nothing for you today, I'm afraid.'

'Actually, I'm calling to sign off.'

'Sign off? What do you mean sign off?'

'I'm away for nine days,' Chamath said. 'When I come back I don't think I'll be working for you any more.'

'*Norton, you can't be serious!*'

'Yes I am.'

'Norton, Norton! You're one of the best in the business, did I ever tell you that?'

No you didn't, Chamath thought. Too late now.

'People love you, especially the voice. A *fuckable* voice, one woman called it!' He chuckled.

Chamath cleared his throat. 'So that's it, I'm afraid.'

'Norton, don't be hasty. Please. Won't you reconsider?'

Chamath remained silent, holding the phone.

'You're going to regret it, I know,' said Gary. He paused. Then his voice became suddenly brisk, conspiratorial. 'Norton, I never make this offer to anybody, but I'm going to make it to you. If you ever, I mean *ever,* change your mind and decide to come back, just call. All right?'

'Sure.'

'*There'll always be an opening for you.*' He chortled. 'You heard what I just said?'

'I heard,' Chamath said and hung up.

They couldn't get three seats together on the plane. There were two to one side, and a single one across the aisle. 'I'll have the single,' said Stelios. 'You sit with her.' Chamath and Elena found themselves next to an enormous individual in sarong and sandals sitting in the window seat.

'My name is Gunapala,' he said crossly. 'I'm from Coulsdon.'

Elena tucked herself into a travel blanket and put her earphones on.

'Is this *suddhi* your wife?' asked Mr Gunapala.

'She's not my wife,' said Chamath.

'Quite right,' said Mr Gunapala. 'I never travel with my wife either. In fact, when I came to Coulsdon I left them all behind in Colombo.'

The steward went past checking their seatbelts.

'I go back once a year,' Mr Gunapala said generously. 'I bring them presents. For my sister, my brother-in-law, my aunties. Even my wife. You know I brought her an epilator last time? You think she's happy? Ha!' He sat there seething in indignation.

Across the aisle Stelios had got hold of a stewardess. 'What do I have to do around here to get a drink?' he asked.

She smiled coyly at him. 'We'll be serving once we're in the air.'

His eyes followed her rear as she swished her way up the aisle in her peacock blue Air Lanka sari. 'Make mine a Bloody Mary,' he called out.

'Your brother's very loud, isn't he?' said Mr Gunapala.

'He's not my brother.'

'Quite right,' said Mr Gunapala approvingly. He looked from one of them to the other. 'Anyway, you're much, *much* darker than him. Have you tried *Fair & Lovely*?'

'No,' said Chamath. 'Now that you mention it, maybe I'll give it a go.'

And so they settled in for the non-stop flight to Colombo, Stelios getting more and more raucous as the empty Bloody Mary cups rolled about on his tray.

'He's impossible on planes,' Elena whispered.

Surreptitiously, Chamath reached out and took her hand underneath the blanket.

At Katunayake he called home from the airport. No answer. Very odd, he thought. His father usually got up at the crack of dawn; in any case, the two elderly women servants who looked after him would be there, Poppy and Sita.

He could see his two friends wilting in the morning heat on the interminable ride into Colombo. They drove past open air stalls where pork joints hung on hooks, casually dripping blood on the roadside; and rows of wrought-iron stands displaying cement flower pots for sale; and innumerable one-man bicycle repair shops. Already the road was choked with traffic, the early morning commuters coming into the city to work, and the dust particles floating in the air were luminous with the promise of the fierce heat to come. His friends' faces looked haggard in the tropical light. He looked away.

His father lived in the smallest of houses, at a particularly hazardous corner of Flower Terrace, alongside an open storm drain into which many an unwitting motorist had driven when they took the corner too sharply. They got down in the front yard and he knocked on the dusty teak front door with the little red census sticker stuck to the lintel above.

After an age Poppy answered. 'Hamu!' she said

in shock. 'Why didn't you tell us you were coming?' Behind her in the gloom of the interior he could see Sita emerge from the kitchen quarters, wiping her hands on her cloth. And then the door to the bedroom opened and his father stepped out, and Chamath stood there in shock: a shrunken old man, his cheeks grizzled with four days' growth of beard. He breathed heavily as he walked.

'My boy,' he said. 'You're here.'

'These are my friends,' Chamath said. 'This is Elena; this is Stelios.'

Chamath's father shook their hands. 'How do you do,' he said listlessly. There was an awkward pause. Chamath stole a look at the dining table. His father had always been a great traditionalist, believing in the big Sri Lankan breakfast: hoppers or stringhoppers or pittu. He would come to table sharp at nine every morning, showered and shaved even if he had nothing else to do that day. It was a little after nine now and there was nothing on the table.

'Ask them if they would like some tea,' he said to Chamath, speaking as if the others were not present. Then he got up. 'If you'll excuse me, I'll go and give Aelian a call. He ought to be up by now.' He disappeared into the bedroom.

Chamath told Sita to pour some tea. He turned to Poppy. 'Where's the breakfast?' he whispered.

'We've stopped making breakfast for quite a while now. Ever since he fell ill.'

'Ill?'

She pointed to her throat. 'He's cured now. He did the course at Maharagama.'

'Maharagama?' he asked, a chill slicing through his heart with exquisite sharpness.

Poppy nodded. 'He forbade me to mention it to anyone. Especially you.'

He understood now the weight loss, the ageing. Hard to think it was the same man who had been in London six months ago, buying flats, playing hell.

'There was no one to drive him; he would go to the hospital in a tuk tuk twice a week on his own for the chemo.' Her eyes misted over. 'When he came back he was so weak Sita and I would have to lift him out. He had no appetite, of course. It killed his appetite.'

'And now?'

'The course is finished. He's OK, they say. But still he won't eat.' She turned her head. Chamath's father came scuttling out of the bedroom with a curious crablike motion Chamath had never seen before.

'Right, it's all fixed. He's expecting you now. 2, Shrubbery Gardens, Bambalapitiya. Over on the seaside.'

'Why didn't you tell me you were ill?' Chamath blurted out.

His father looked startled. 'I'm fine now,' he said with an attempt at brightness.

'Can I see the reports?'

'Reports?' the old man eyed him suspiciously. 'What reports?'

'The medical reports,' Chamath said patiently. 'Can I see them?'

'Oh, *those* reports.' A look of extreme cunning flickered across his face. 'Oh dear me, no. They're between me and my doctor, you see. They're confidential.'

I'm your son, Chamath wanted to cry out. *I have a right to see them. I only want to help!* But he knew this was the least valid of reasons in his father's canon. He could not keep the bitterness out of his voice. 'The Kumarihamy, or Poppy or Sita,' he said, 'any of them could have told me you were ill. They had a duty.'

The old man's eyes flashed imperiously. 'Their loyalties are to *me*, not you, understand?' He looked towards Elena and Stelios. 'And might I thank you not to discuss the very private matter of my health in front of strangers?'

'Strangers?' Chamath rose to his feet, and a lifetime of frustration and hopelessness and sheer anger rose in him like floodwater at monsoon. '*Strangers?*'

His friends moved nervously in their chairs and he motioned for them to wait outside. He stood, his face six inches from his father's, towering over his shrunken frame. 'They're not strangers!' he yelled. 'They're the closest thing to a family *I* will ever have.'

He stood there for a second, for the full meaning of his words to sink in. Then he turned and left.

He was angry with himself for getting angry. He thought: Why do we expect such high standards from our own that we don't from outsiders? Especially when we know only too well how short of them they will fall? He was angry with his father for no longer being the good-looking man in his prime who had left London a few months ago. He was angry because there was nothing he could do about it: he could not rewind time to bring him back.

Inconsequentially, and rather absurdly, he thought of Mr Gunapala from the plane. Did he notice the difference in his wife every year when he came back home? (Apart from her being less hairy, that is.) Did it seem to him that he was fast-forwarding her life with the remote control in his hand, seeing her for just one week or whatever it was every year? And if so, did he feel the anguish of that?

'Your father's a good man,' Elena said gently. 'He didn't want you worrying. You had enough on your plate.'

'He's selfish and vain,' Chamath said angrily. 'He didn't want me to see him like this out of sheer vanity. And selfish, because by doing this he's caused me even more grief.'

'It's not as if you could have dropped everything and come back,' she pointed out. 'You were in the middle of your appeal.'

'He wasn't to know that.'

'At least you have a father,' Stelios said quietly. 'Mine left home when I was too young to remember. My mother refuses to talk about him. He could be a Martian for all I know.'

Chamath looked at his friends. We are all halves and thirds and quarters, he thought sadly. Maybe that's why we only seem to add up to a whole when we're together.

The lessons in Swing were not turning out to be a success. The Beast was so big and the room so small that dancing with him was a life-threatening exercise. The first day the Sacred Heart lamp went sailing through the air, landing with a crash somewhere near the kitchen corridor. They replaced it. The next day the Sacred Heart picture itself came crashing down. They took it to Cheap Deals to reframe. The day after that he broke it again.

'Really, Don, anyone would think you were anti-Catholic,' said Bar fondly.

The reason for Don coming to their house every evening was becoming increasingly clear to Ginnie: it was not for Bar, whatever she might think; it was not out of boredom or loneliness; and it was certainly not for the dancing. She wondered about this curious concept of love: how could it mean so many different things to so many different people?

Did Don have any idea of what he meant when he whispered under his breath 'I love you' as he kissed her hand under the mango tree every evening? He had never been in a relationship before, of that she was fairly sure. So could you then suddenly fall in love in your sixties? And what were *her* feelings on the matter?

She was fond of him in a way you might be fond of your teddy bear. Or the way they had been fond of Daddy. But love?

And then there was the vexing question of Him upstairs. He had not said one word or done a single thing to justify her intuition. But there was something about Him, something so familiar yet alien, that drew her to him. Had she met him before? It was almost as if she had known him from another life, though this was patently absurd. I must be more like Bar, she told herself: charming and soignée, totally practical, totally ruthless. Bar who would never let a little thing like love get in the way of a big thing like life.

The van turned in through the wrought-iron gates on Galle Road and bumped down a leafy drive, ending up at the verandah of a long low single-storey house, with two wings on either side which swooped in to form a forecourt. A tall figure bounded down the three steps to greet them.

'Welcome to Sri Lanka!' he said. 'My name,' he puffed out his chest slightly, is 'Aelian de Silva, the Ginger Beer King of Bambalapitiya. And this'—he extended a sweeping hand behind him—'is Bubbles!' Behind the house, where the land sloped gently down, you could glimpse the ocean, a strip of turquoise against the shimmering white of the sky. He turned back and pointed to the front garden. 'You will be staying in that cottage over there.' The three of them looked at the pretty art deco villa that stood to one side of the main gate, at the corner of Shrubbery Gardens and Galle Road.

'But first you must come in and sample a little of our famous Sri Lankan hospitality.'

His friends were exhausted—he could see them exchanging looks—but there was no way to say no politely. They went inside, into the gloom of two enormous reception rooms separated by a gigantic arch. Standing guard on either side of the arch were two of the biggest elephant tusks they had ever seen—six foot at least—mounted in ebony.

'Ginnie! Bar!' Mr de Silva clapped his hands. 'My daughters,' he explained. 'Never there when you want them. All over you when you don't.' There were scuffles and giggles from the nearest bedroom off the main hall, but nobody came out.

'Ginger beer for four! And make it quick, these poor people are dying of thirst!'

A maid scurried up to them with a chromium tray on which were four glasses, painted in black and white swirls, filled with foaming ginger beer. (In true traditional style she served the men first.)

'I sold the business,' Aelian said, as if that was what they had been discussing before the maid came in. 'So the ginger beer you are drinking is, alas, no longer my own.' He smiled, a crafty smile that seemed to have sneaked onto his face without his permission, and lowered his voice. 'There were debts, you see.'

Chamath was reminded of his own father. How similar they were, these gentlemen of a certain age, all graduates of the same school of cunning! 'So you know my father?' he asked.

'Of course I know Raja.' Aelian put a hand to his heart. 'Terrible business, that. His sisters in Kandy, and no one here to look after him.' He looked at Chamath, suddenly realizing what he had said. 'Well of course you're here, now.' He smiled, a little unconvincingly.

'If you don't mind, we'd like to go to our rooms,' Chamath said getting up.

'Yes, yes, I'll show you the place.'

Putting on a battered solar topee that was lined in bright, billiard-table-green cloth, he led the way down a sandy path, between bushes of oleander and frangipani and wild jasmine, to a pretty grill door which he unlocked. There was a small sparsely furnished sitting room with two bedrooms leading off, and adjoining them a shared bathroom. Beyond was a narrow passage which served as a kitchen.

'I have plans,' said Aelian de Silva, 'to put up an annexe above the garage. In good time, all in good time!' You could see the good ideas fizzing and foaming one after the other in his mind even if the ginger beer business was gone. 'I know you'll be very comfortable here, and if there's anything you want, Gin and Bar will be only too happy to oblige.' He turned to Chamath. 'And will you be staying here with them or going back to your father's?'

The question hung in the air, pregnant with implication.

'I'll be here,' Chamath said shortly.

They had not slept for over twenty-four hours but they were beyond tiredness now, the way a marathon runner must feel after the first ten miles. Stelios pushed the two iron beds together, with their lumpy coir mattresses. 'Come on,' he said. 'What are we waiting for?'

21

Chamath gently extricated himself from the tangle of limbs in the bed. The air was heavy with the smell of sweat and sex and frangipani blossom, and he felt dizzy and light-headed. Was it lack of food? Or was it emotional exhaustion? Quietly he padded across to the bathroom. There was a square red cement shower tray but the head of the shower appeared to be missing. At knee level there was a tap in the wall, and a red plastic bucket. Filling it he sluiced himself down, watching the little runnels of water trickle down his legs and between his toes, washing away the sins of half a year. There was a cake of bright pink carbolic soap on the window ledge. Soaping himself he looked out at the low old house. A girl came out of it and stood in front, one of Aelian's daughters. She looked uncannily like a Sri Lankan version of Elena, masses of frizzy hair and a nose in line with her forehead. He realized with a shock she was looking straight at him, his naked self framed in the bars of the window—a cool gaze, bold in its impudence. They stood this way, locked together for a long moment, each unwilling to move, till finally he tore himself away and stepped back. He wondered which it was, Ginnie or Bar? He finished his bath, toweling himself dry with the very rough scrap of cloth provided. He couldn't see the sea from this window but he felt it: the bold brassy notes suddenly swelling and muting under the tinny whine of Galle Road. He breathed in the late afternoon sunlight; and the sea air soft with sand so fine and powdery you only felt it once it was in your nostrils.

Pulling on a pair of shorts and T-shirt he crept out of the house and up Shrubbery Gardens, catching the bus on Galle Road to Colpetty. He surrendered to the moist warmth of its interior, the feeling that he and his fellow passengers were packed carefully between layers of damp cotton wool. The window glass was brown with grime, the chromium handrail sticky to the touch; the jagged tears in the rexine seat covers pricked his bare thighs. He was excited by this seediness: charged by its vibrancy and liveliness in a way he had never been by the seediness of Kensal Green. Getting off at Colpetty Junction he cut through the side streets of his childhood, Milepost Avenue, Palm Grove and Clifford Road. Negotiating the storm drain he arrived at Flower Terrace.

'Your father's still asleep,' Poppy said. 'He's not got up from his afternoon nap.'

'It's you I came to see. I need the details of his doctor.'

'Dr Daluwatte,' she said rapidly, as if she had been practising for weeks this quick transfer of information. 'Aloe Avenue, Colpetty. I'll get you the number.'

He vaguely knew Aloe Avenue. It ran parallel to Shrubbery Gardens, a mile further north. Before Poppy had time to return, the door to his father's room opened. There stood for a moment, framed against the darkness inside, an unknown man, small, stooped and slightly furtive: the stranger on the train. Then recognition kicked in and the stranger became his father.

'So you're back? Come, sit.'

Sita brought them tea and they sat facing the front yard with its high hedges of ixora and croton, a small green room into which the pale late afternoon sunlight filtered, bleached of strength and colour like an ageing coloured photograph. They sat in silence a long time. For Chamath it was always the most melancholic time of day, when the lights went out one by one, as if on a hundred silent switches.

'You have to remember,' the old man said, 'that your life is your own. You cannot live yours through mine, and I cannot live mine through yours. I cannot,' he shifted slightly in his chair for emphasis, 'I *will* not have you making a martyr of yourself for any cause. Least of all mine.'

It's not a cause, Chamath thought. You're my father: I would have taken the next plane home.

'I believe I have set you up well,' his father continued. 'Your job is to pick up the ball and run with it. *And not look back.*'

There was something Chamath had always wanted— needed—to ask: 'You wrote me a letter once, saying you could no longer afford to support me. Did you really mean it? Surely you didn't mean it? Was it a knee-jerk reaction to the cancer?' But in the fading light he found his courage had faded too, and he remained silent. The answer might have been important once: so much had happened to each of them since, the question was purely academic now, the answer irrelevant. The time for recriminations and *what ifs* was long gone.

Almost as they watched, the green room turned to silver, then purple, then black: the fast-forward of a tropical sunset. Chamath could barely see his father's features now. It made it that much easier; he could imagine the father he was used to, not this shrunken stranger.

'Bring your friends to lunch tomorrow,' the old man said abruptly.

'We're taking the inter-city to Kandy early morning,' Chamath replied, a little reluctantly. 'We won't be back till evening.'

The old man said nothing. There was no talk of being invited another time. Perhaps as things stood now, his father could only think of one day at a time.

'I brought you this,' Chamath said. He gave him the duty-free bag with the bottle of cognac in it. Every morning his father took his coffee with cognac and a raw egg beaten into it. Did he still do that now?

'Thank you.' The old man briefly looked inside the bag and put it down by his side. There was another long silence. It settled into the space between them, moist and palpable, like a furry tropical night insect.

'So I'll go then, shall I?' Chamath said after a while. But the old man was lost in the darkness, in a world far away, and there was no answer.

As he left the house, Poppy pushed a small piece of paper into his hand, the number of the doctor. I am back inside the green maze, Chamath thought. How could I have ever imagined I had escaped? The monster was only around the corner, large and juicy and quivering, waiting patiently for its meat.

Early next morning, at the ungodly hour of 7.10 they set off for Kandy. He and Stelios sat on the steps of the open carriage, the mountains and valleys laid out before them in one dramatic sweep after another.

'The finest thing the British did,' Chamath said. 'Not the tea, not the schools, not the law. Just this: the railway.'

In Kandy he showed them the ancestral house, the Walauwa, now barred and padlocked. 'My father sold it to send me abroad,' he explained. 'You can imagine how much of a sacrifice it must have been for him. I am not sure I would go that far for my kids.'

'So who's there now?' she asked.

'A tyre manufacturer,' he said smiling. 'Kandy is now mostly owned by tyre manufacturers.'

They visited the Temple of the Tooth, the Buddhist holy of holies where the tooth of the Lord Buddha was preserved. 'Yes,' said Stelios. He showed them the exquisitely painted eighteenth-century roof timbers of the old palace. 'Yes,' said Stelios, 'yes, yes.' He showed them the windowless room where the treasures of the kingdom—the tributes to the King—had been stored, and to which his ancestor had had the key.

Stelios looked at the empty room. 'So where's it all gone then?'

'I don't know,' he replied with a grin. 'We're still digging.'

And finally, yellow rice and chicken curry with all trimmings at that bastion of colonial degustation—the Queen's Hotel—before the afternoon train back.

'The beach!' cried Stelios. 'For God's sake somebody please, *please* get me to the beach!'

Bar and Ginnie couldn't wait to get in. They knew the hours of the Kandy train. They knew they had the whole day. Bar produced the spare key and opened the padlock on the pretty art deco grill door. The house had lain unoccupied for many years, an uneasy reminder of Ginnie's as yet unrealized future. Somehow it felt different now, with people in it. Underneath the ever-present salt sea air they could detect notes of another presence: atavistic and animal, raw and sensual; a presence that could easily overpower you if you didn't consciously ignore it.

'Oh look, dear, they've pushed the beds together!' Ginnie began bouncing up and down on the creaky bed springs. The bed in the next room appeared to be unoccupied. They pondered this development awhile. Ginnie thought of the man with the soap all over him, unable to take his eyes off her. She said nothing.

'He's just the tour guide,' Bar explained. 'I saw him go off in a pair of shorts last afternoon. *Shorts*, can you imagine? Probably went home to the slums of Wanathamulla. Bet you he has tattoos in unmentionable places.'

Having solved this mystery they set about trying on the various sundresses and bikinis of the foreign girl.

'She looks a bit like me, don't you think?'

'Don't flatter yourself, dear. You're much, *much* darker. Besides, those clothes won't fit you. You are— how can I put this nicely?—just a *leetle* bit larger.'

With some difficulty Ginnie managed to struggle

into the coffee brown bikini. 'There you are! What do you say to that?'

'Oh, take it off! You're making the frangipani blush. You're embarrassing me, you're probably embarrassing your future husband!'

'But I don't *have* a future husband, that's the problem!'

'Are you surprised? The way *you're* carrying on!'

Chamath ran along the beach. It was early in the morning and it felt good to be alone, however briefly. Living with other people—and it was the first time he had been so completely and continuously in their presence— it was interesting how even your thoughts were no longer your own. There was a collective process at work, a sort of gang mentality whose thoughts and words were different—from your singular thoughts and actions, to which you reverted only when you were physically alone.

At certain points he had to clamber over huge boulders dumped on the beach to prevent erosion. He had barely run half a mile and already he was bathed in sweat. He regretted having worn a tracksuit, but you could hardly turn up to meet a cancer specialist in running shorts.

'Come early,' Dr Daluwatte had said. 'Before the patients arrive.'

After several false turns inland from the beach he

found Aloe Avenue. Panting, he rang the bell. The doctor himself opened the door. 'I must say this is all highly irregular, Mr Pilimatalawa.'

'Call me Chamath.'

'It's a breach of doctor–patient confidentiality. But I will make an exception in this case since you are only here for a short time.' The doctor sighed. 'You are his next of kin, after all.'

Chamath waited in silence, hardly daring to open his mouth, his heart beating violently. From the run, of course.

'Your father has, *had*, cancer of the pharynx. The good news is that being in the throat it was easy to treat in isolation. I put him on an intense course of radio and chemo.' The doctor paused. 'Although he is in his 60s your father is a tough man. Quite often in such cases the cure will virtually kill you even if the disease doesn't. And he survived.'

'So is he in the clear?' Chamath asked.

'Understand this. With cancer you are never entirely in the clear.' The doctor paused. 'But in this case I am very optimistic it's completely under control. I have asked him to come in for a check-up in three months' time. After that, once every six months.'

Chamath's eyes welled up with tears. 'I can't thank you enough, Doctor.'

'So you can go back to England with a clear conscience.'

Chamath rose. 'Just one last thing,' he said. 'Would it have helped if I had been here?'

The doctor looked at him curiously. 'That was the first thing I asked him. Whether he had any family member who could accompany him to treatments, who could be there for him. But you see, Chamath, we humans tend to forget that underneath this spurious intellectual cover we are, first and last, animals. When an animal is dying it doesn't surround itself with other animals. It crawls into a hole and waits for death. Alone.

'Your father thought he was going to die. He didn't want to have to deal with all the paraphernalia, the soul searching, the intellectual hype that we insist on surrounding ourselves with at death. To have you here would have meant all that. He would have had all the stress of putting up a front purely for your benefit. He decided otherwise.' The doctor paused. 'It was his choice. So don't beat yourself up about it.'

They had hired a small shack—no more than four walls and a roof, with an outhouse lavatory—at one end of the bay. Unawatuna had just been voted one of the ten most beautiful bays in the world. Protected by a coral reef it had just the right type of waves—it was the time of the south-west monsoon—and just the right amount of semi-naked tourists to keep Stelios happy. In 1980, Unawatuna was topless and virtually bottomless.

'Cor, look at that!' Stelios said. 'My God, look at the pair on that!' He became the life and soul of the party, the man everyone on that small bay knew; the one everyone wanted to know.

It left Chamath and Elena to fend for each other. He watched her, covertly at first, because there was something so 'shocking' about seeing her topless in public. His innate Sri Lankan prudishness kicked in; and then he was ashamed of his shame. At the same time he was shocked by her loveliness: the small perfect breasts burnt caramel by the sun, the mass of frizzy blonde hair that refused to be tamed even by the waves, the low slung hips in their brown bikini bottoms. It made him proud to think she was all his—at least half his—in the secrecy of the night.

She watched Stelios's antics with indulgent amusement.

'How do you cope?' he asked curiously.

'Oh, it stopped bothering me a long time ago.'

'Haven't you ever confronted him about it? Sat him down and explained how much it affects you?'

'I just told you, it *doesn't* bother me.'

'Doesn't it?'

She sighed, and he could see she was annoyed with

him. 'You have a lot to learn, don't you, about other people's marriages. First thing, you don't question what goes on inside them.'

He was stung. Again she had chosen to draw a circle in the sand around herself and Stelios. So I suppose I shouldn't question their motives for having *me* around either, he thought angrily.

But in spite of her words he could see she followed her husband's erratic and erotic progress up the beach with close attention. And there was something about Stelios's high good humour, the irrepressible blatancy of his flirtation that was almost impossible to get angry with. He was like the child whose antics got naughtier and naughtier in front of his parents just to see how far he could push the limits: you almost felt he wouldn't bother if he knew his wife wasn't watching.

'Oh, he'll never leave me,' she said almost defiantly. Chamath put a consoling hand over hers, to show that he accepted her wisdom on these matters, however flawed it seemed to him.

She turned to him. 'Let's talk about you.' She began asking endless questions about his early life in Sri Lanka. She was fascinated by his somewhat curious upbringing.

'And what did *you* think when you first saw me?' he asked in turn.

'I thought you were some sort of prince. A prince who had lost his way, but was too proud to ask directions. You had such a haughty bearing, so distant. There was this other-worldly look in your eyes.'

He laughed. 'Then you saw me in my real surroundings next day, and that was that.'

'It only increased my love for you.'

'Love? Be honest. Was it love or was it pity?'

'Don't you think at my age I can be trusted to tell the difference?'

'Don't ever pity me,' he said hotly. 'I couldn't bear that.'

'You know how much we both love you,' she repeated gently.

This easy use of the word *love* bothered him. Between them they used it so often on him. *I love you. How we love you! You are the one we most love in this world.* It was an embarrassment of riches he found hard to digest, coming as he did from a family that had always used its praises so sparingly, with such great parsimony.

Later he would think to himself, bitterly and cynically, that it must have been the cotton wool of that word in which he was rolled so generously and liberally that bought them his loyalty: a loyalty he would take with him to the grave.

Was it one big con? Was it generosity, misplaced and insincere? Was it pity? Or did they—God help us all—actually mean it?

22

There was no air-conditioning in the shack, just a wobbly fan corroded by sea air. Often he would creep out at night to escape the heat—leaving the others to their gentle sleep—to sit on the banked sand under the coconut tree, watching the waves roll in one after the other in the silver-blue moonlight. The way ahead was baffling now, too many paths available to him, too many options. In a perverse way he almost wished for that time not so long ago when he was still below the grid, at home in that underworld of his own choosing where the monsters were contemptible yet familiar, ugly but lovable. Thanks or no thanks to his father's troubles, the Kandyan princess had receded into the background: she might still make her grand entrance, but it seemed that now was neither the time nor the place. You're just in a hurry to get back to your sex games in Wimbledon, he said to himself. You can't wait to get it out, can you?

For no reason at all he thought of Jamila. I must touch base with her as soon as I get back. Directly or not, I owe my freedom to her. He had been too wrapped up in his own anguish to spare her even a moment of thought. I really am a fair-weather friend, he thought hopelessly. Now that I am respectable again, I can go back to having respectable friends. Why did she keep wanting to see me these last few weeks?

Another figure came out and slid silently onto the sand next to him. They continued looking out at the sea for a long time, immersed in the deep of it, the hush and whisper of its waves.

'What are you thinking?' Stelios asked.

'About what I'm going to do next,' Chamath murmured.

'Go back to what you do best,' he said without hesitation. 'Be a professional. Loads of money. Great lifestyle. Work when you want, sleep when you want.'

Yes, Chamath thought. And I'll be riddled with disease and dead in the gutter by thirty.

'Or let's live on this beach,' Stelios said. 'You and me, we don't need much, eh? By day we'll catch fish. By night we'll fuck the girls.'

He lay back on the sand and looked up at the stars. Chamath looked at his friend's features, cut with a chisel out of the silver-blue moonlight. It was the most tempting offer anyone had made in a long time. But then he thought of Elena, and the fact that this future didn't somehow seem to include her. He thought of her words back then, when she hardly knew him: *Stelios has a way of destroying what he loves best, what is most dear to him.*

On the last day they were eating fish and chips at their local, The Happy Banana, when a familiar figure walked past.

'Hello there,' Chamath said smiling.

It was Mr Gunapala with a Russian dolly bird on either arm, sporting an enormous hairy belly and a pair of lemon-yellow budgie smugglers which, sadly, revealed rather more than they concealed.

'This is Masha,' he said, 'and this is,' he looked enquiringly at the other girl, 'Kasha?'

'But which of them is your wife?' Chamath asked.

Mr Gunapala looked shocked. 'Neither,' he said. 'They're *suddhis!*' Obviously the two concepts were mutually exclusive. He looked disapprovingly at Stelios. 'Your brother's getting very black, isn't he? Tell him to try *Boiled and Beautiful*,' he said. '*Fair and Lovely* doesn't seem to be doing the trick.'

Chamath grinned. 'So how's it going so far, Mr Gunapala? How's the family?'

Mr Gunapala bristled at the question. 'I brought her a three-speed drill with a diamond tip,' he said. 'I bought her a *motorcycle* helmet. You think she's happy?' With an indignant wave of the hand he walked on.

On the way to the airport they stopped one last time at Flower Terrace. Chamath hugged his father, feeling the soft bristles of his unshaven cheek, the slight odour of old age seeping out from under his ribcage. Be strong, he told himself. Turn the page. *Carry on reading, the book's not finished yet.*

The old man looked sharply at Elena and Stelios as if seeing them for the very first time. 'So *you're* his friends?' He shook his head almost theatrically. 'Brings them to this country, keeps them hidden. Doesn't even bring them home for a meal. Really, the way my son behaves!'

'We'll be back,' Stelios said, winking at Chamath as he said it. 'We'll be back, won't we?'

Bar and Ginnie were sorry to see them go. Daddy so rarely allowed tourists to occupy the house—never mind that they so badly needed the money!—it was a high point in their humdrum lives when he did. Gin, especially, felt she had got to know the Spanish girl really rather well. Oh, she hadn't actually said one single word to her, but nothing endears you to another person so much as prancing around in her bikini, with your sister shouting hysterically behind you, 'Off! Off! Take it off!' You really feel you know what it's like to be in their shoes; sort of.

On the question of the men they were strictly divided.

'I like the Greek, oh I like the Greek!' breathed Bar.

'Cypriot, dear. Apparently he's Greek Cypriot.'

'*You* know what I mean.'

'Actually, I can't help having a leetle soft spot for the tour guide.'

'Ginnie, you *can't* be serious! Think of the tattoos!'

'I am,' said Ginnie sorrowfully. 'I am. The tattoos are what I'm thinking of.'

The old man stopped typing and massaged his wrist. The physical pain was slight. It was the mental pain that kept him going. How it hurt him to think that Aelian de Silva's daughter had not even recognized him, all those years later when he came to be interviewed by them as a prospective lodger! But why should she? It had been thirty-five years ago. They had never even spoken to each other. Just one look from the bathroom window that long-ago afternoon. It gave him a sort of strange power, having that knowledge of her without her knowledge of it: he was like a peeping tom standing in the dark outside the lighted room, watching her move about inside. The prize.

It was bound to happen. All this running about with dogs in the monsoon rains. Ginnie caught a severe cold.

'I think, dear, a good dose of coriander water will set you to rights.'

'You know how I *hate* coriander water.'

'Try and be a little grown-up about this dear. You know how I *hate* it when Don steps on my toes during the foxtrot. Do you hear me complaining?'

'I thought, perhaps, an antibiotic?'

'*Antibiotic?* What on earth would Daddy say?'

Neither of them knew how to boil up a pot of coriander water. Luckily for them the next day was Sakuntala's day. Sakuntala had never boiled coriander water in her life either, coming as she did from her Wanathamulla tenement where they only believed in erythromycin, augmentin and selexid, but she was daring enough to give tradition a try.

They forced it down Ginnie's throat.

'Really, dear, anyone would think we were trying to kill you.'

'You are, I *know* you are. I'm sure you're after this house.'

'What a thing to say. Just because Daddy felt there was no way to get you married off without a house!'

'You know perfectly well he was going to build you the identical one at the other end of the garden. He just ran out of money, that's all.'

They felt a little better after this skirmish.

Unfortunately the cold got a lot worse. It went down into the chest.

'A doctor!' Ginnie cried. 'Please, *please* get me to a doctor.'

'I've done one better,' said Bar. 'I've called Don.'

'In Antioch the weather was so *wunnerful* we never got colds,' said Don. Which really didn't help matters at all. And so it had to be hospital. But wait a minute. It wasn't as simple as that.

'What hospital, dear?'

'Oh, I think Durdans, don't you? Daddy always swore by Durdans.'

'I thought Daddy always swore *at* Durdans!'

So they decided on Asiri.

'And I will sit with you morning, noon and night till you're well. I won't leave your side,' threatened Bar. 'It'll prove to you I'm not after your house.'

'Then who will look after Shorts?'

'Then who will look after Shorts?' echoed Bar a little foolishly.

They thought for a while. 'I know. Don!' But this idea had certain acute disadvantages.

'He's always putting his own dog on a diet. *He weighs his food!*'

'Shorts will wither away and die,' said Bar. 'I can't deal with two deaths in the family.'

'I knew it!' cried Ginnie triumphantly. 'I knew it! I just *knew* you were expecting me to die!'

A little while later the old man heard a tapping at his door. He was surprised to see that Bar had hauled herself up the staircase to his entrance.

'My sister's not well and I have to take her to hospital.'

'Unwell?' he asked in alarm. 'What's wrong with her?'

'A heavy cold which has turned into bronchitis. I'm taking her to Asiri. We have a great favour to ask of you.'

And so it was that the old man found himself having to go downstairs twice a day to put dog food into Shorts's bowl. Not forgetting, of course, the daily dog walk on Marine Drive.

23

It was the tail-end of August when they flew in to London. The first thing they did back at the flat was to open the windows. The big-city air felt stale and used; what you needed was to open the windows onto London itself.

'Did you enjoy it?' he asked them uncertainly. He knew it had not been an unqualified success. He thought of the heat and the flies and the mosquitoes. He thought of Flower Terrace, and how he had been unable to offer what even the poorest Sri Lankan would have unhesitatingly offered visiting friends: a meal in his own home.

She touched his arm. 'It was perfect,' she said quietly. And he was grateful for this gentle lie: the words were there as evidence, bold and unreliable, even if the sentiments were not.

'Man, that Unawatuna!' said Stelios. 'You think by

next year it might go completely nude? You think we should go back and start the trend?'

It took so little to keep Stelios happy, he thought with a smile. Why can't I be like that? Why must I have this divine discontent, this exquisite ache inside of me all the time? Why must I rise above and beyond this mortal body to observe and judge, so that my pleasures are never unalloyed, my pains always tempered with the cold water of reason? Why can't I live like other people with the colour turned up on my life?

As if to illustrate the point, Stelios said: 'Right, who's for the carnival, then?'

They looked at him in silent incomprehension.

'The Notting Hill Carnival,' he said, as if explaining to two infants. 'Have you forgotten?'

'Chamath, you want to go with him?' she said. 'I have too much unpacking to do.'

He hesitated. 'I'll stay, shall I?'

'Wimp!' said Stelios. 'Right, I'm off. See you when I see you.'

'He's better out of the way,' she said when he was gone. 'If he's here, on the pretext of helping he'll make even more of a mess. That's what happens when you force him to do something he really doesn't want to.'

Chamath hung his few things in the hall cupboard. He unpacked the pound of tea in its silver foil—single estate—that he had brought for Jamila as a present.

The phone rang, a call from Spain, and he could hear Elena speaking incredibly fast, an unending stream of Spanish consonants. He went into the kitchen to load the washing machine and stopped to admire his handiwork: the golden kitchen which seemed to float now, lustrous and light over the solid black floor. If I've given them nothing else I've given them this, he thought happily. He opened a bottle of Rioja and poured himself a generous glass. How far away his father and Poppy and Sita seemed now. It was easy to forget they even existed. All that mattered was the here and the now: the water had flowed in to fill the container and assume its shape: he was supremely content within the warmth and glow of this small-time domesticity.

'My father sends his love,' Elena said coming into the kitchen. 'He's dying to meet you. I told him how green your country was—he couldn't believe it. Where we come from it's so brown all year round, almost desert.'

They took the bottle and glasses to their favourite place on the carpet under the open window, and the summer air hovered over them, burnt and breathless, hungry for any new development.

'So,' she said turning to him. 'What next?'

'You tell me,' he murmured.

'I want to take you to Madrid,' she said. 'There's a club there called the Ola Ola Club. I can picture you there, dressed all in white, with your dark skin. They'll go crazy for you.'

But the wine was working inside him and all he wanted was to take her in his arms. My desires lie closer to home, he wanted to say, not in Spain. Taboos are meant to be broken. But he held back. For honour and loyalty and decency and plain good sense: all those reasons which mean so much at that precise moment; and so little when you look back upon them years later.

It was late. They were too drunk to cook. He went downstairs to the end of the road to get fish and chips. He was rooting about inside the newspaper parcel on the way back, trying to fish out a chip or two, when he bumped into her. For a moment he failed to recognize the huge halo of fuzzy red hair.

'Jamila!' he said. 'What on earth are *you* doing here?'

She looked startled. 'Looking for a friend. Couldn't find the address.'

He couldn't believe he was seeing her here on this road, so far off her beat. 'So, how are you?' he asked. He felt a little foolish because the two of them had long ago passed this how-are-you stage.

'I'm good,' she said. 'I'm good.' It was as if they were both of them in some amateur dramatic society in a parish hall, at the first read-through.

'It's so hot, isn't it?' he said looking around.

'Yes it is,' she agreed. 'Hot.'

He was bursting to tell her about his travels. 'I've just come back from Sri Lanka,' he said happily. 'I brought you some tea.' But he made no move to go up and get it. He knew if he did, he would be forced to ask her up, and he was unwilling. There was a certain magic in the air up there: it could so easily vanish if you opened the door too wide and let other people in. So he grinned foolishly and stood there looking at her, not saying anything.

And then she did the strangest thing. Reaching up she pulled his head down and kissed him hard, her tongue fighting its way through his lips and teeth to his tongue. 'Come home,' she whispered fiercely. 'I want you. I *need* you.'

It was so unexpected it threw him off balance. 'Jamila!' he said. 'What are you *doing?*' Involuntarily he pushed her away, wiping the lip gloss from his mouth with the back of his hand. But she was holding onto his arm now, pulling him towards her with surprising force. He shook his hand to free it. He had been living so long within the bounds of that other country he had forgotten the geography of this one: it was as if a complete stranger on the streets had thrown herself at him, and all he wanted was to free himself. But in that same moment he realized too the significance of his actions, and instantly regretted them.

He saw the anger blaze up in her eyes. 'Bastard!' she hissed. 'You fucking bastard. I have always, *always* been there for you—you know that. Now, when I need you—'

'Jamila!' he interrupted. 'Since when have you needed *me*?'

She was crying now, in deep hoarse gulps, her chest heaving. He tried to put his arms round her but she pushed him off fiercely. 'Get away from me!' she screamed. 'You no good piece of shit! How could I have ever imagined that you, that I . . .' she shook her head sorrowfully, lost in her own train of thought.

He stood there helplessly, equally sorrowful because the temple goddess had turned out, after all, to be only a fallen idol, just like everyone else. As he watched her he realized there was nowhere he could even take her to, to sit her down and comfort her, because back in the flat upstairs there was another story unfolding, another life about to unravel.

'Jamila,' he said urgently. 'Go home. I'll come and see you tomorrow.' He didn't mention the tea. The time for tea was long past. He was unwilling to leave her on the pavement in the dark all on her own, but the siren call from upstairs was screaming inside his head now: powerful, silent; primal. 'Tomorrow!' he repeated, and bounded up the road praying she wouldn't see which house he went into.

But upstairs, something had happened in his absence. The breathless air of expectation was gone.

'What took you so long?' she asked.

His emotions were all over the place and he couldn't

quite read the note in her voice. 'Long queue at the chippie,' he replied.

Perhaps the anxiety on the pavement below had followed him silently up the carpeted stairs. Perhaps the burnt summer had crept in and taken over, a third unwanted guest at this intimate dinner, garrulous with stale jokes and unreliable laughter. Like a swimmer who loses the rhythm of his stroke through momentary lack of concentration, he floundered, vainly trying to recreate the lost intimacy of only twenty minutes ago. But what he found instead was a different vibe, a different rhythm: the tired good cheer of fellow runners after a race; not the darkly perfumed promise of what could so easily have been. They finished their fish and chips in silence; and the jet lag began to kick in. They left Stelios's portion in the oven.

'Good night,' she said kissing him perfunctorily on the cheek. 'And thank you for a really, really beautiful holiday.'

For a long time he lay awake in his sheets listening to even the most minute sounds coming from the next room, unbearably alive to the fact that they were the only two creatures in this nest under the roof, separated by the thinnest of partitions. He hoped she was listening to every rustle and scuffle on his side; but he wasn't sure.

In spite of the rain the old man walked Shorts faithfully every afternoon. He had barely stepped out of the gate when the familiar sounds of *I say! I say!* assailed his ears. He quickened his steps down the slope to the sea. There was a great pounding of feet behind him.

'I say! You do walk fast, don't you!'

'Do I?' said the old man turning round innocently.

'I went to see the little lady at Asiri this morning,' Don explained. He mispronounced *Asiri*, stressing the middle syllable. For some reason this annoyed the old man intensely.

'It's Ah-siri,' said the old man. 'As in arse.'

But Don wasn't listening. He had his own story to tell. 'She's rather tetchy at the moment, the little lady. I took her a bunch of lilies.

'"Lilies!" she screamed. "Take them away at once! Didn't anyone ever tell you they're the flowers of death? Get them out of here!" So I had to take them outside and give them to the nurses. The other sister, the tiny one, came out and calmed me down. "You see what I have to put up with every day?" she said. "You see how difficult my sister can be?" But she's a plucky one, that Bar, I can tell you. I have nothing but admiration for her!'

The red brick pavement along Marine Drive was not wide enough to take two men and two dogs, so they had to walk single file, and thankfully, conversation became impossible in the fine mist of rain.

I must go and see her, the old man thought.

Next morning he got dressed in his thin white shirt and stripey tie. He didn't know the dress code for hospital visits. On the way he stopped at *Shirohana* and bought a single red long-stemmed rose. He was not one given to the grand gesture, the dramatic flourish: a single flower was just enough, no more.

They gave him the room number at reception and he took the lift up. At the nurse's station in the long corridor he saw the enormous bunch of lilies on the counter-top, brazen and perfumed. The Lilies of Antioch.

He listened outside the door but could hear nothing. Quietly he opened it and peeped in. The patient seemed to be sleeping. By her side was Bar, and next to Bar the Beast. Luckily they hadn't seen him. He quietly withdrew his head, closing the door. So what now?

It was awkward carrying a single thorny rose while you negotiated the crowds outside in Kirula Road, but the old man managed. He got more than a few odd looks. He felt like one of those old-fashioned saints in holy books who are always portrayed with a flower in their hand. He went into a pastry shop and bought a patty and a glass of iced coffee. Laying the rose down carefully on the formica table he ate his frugal supper. It must have been a good hour later when he went back up to the room and this time luck was on his side; it was free of visitors. But the patient was still asleep, and the old man hovered, not really knowing what to do. He looked at those features all too familiar from another time, another place—the masses of frizzy hair, the nose almost in line with the forehead—and his fingers trembled with an urgent desire to trace and re-trace the familiar routes of that terrain, a landscape he knew so well he could have negotiated it blindfolded, in the dark. Instead, feeling a little foolish, he began to wave the rose in her face. This is the moment, he thought sadly, when the princess in the fairytale is so overcome by its deep scent that her eyelids flutter open, and the prince leans over and kisses her to the sublime music of celestial strings. But there was no music. All he could hear was a far-off *Fur Elise*, a one-fingered ringtone rendition by a baker's tuk tuk, advertising fresh loaves for sale; but the patient's eyes remained shut. The rose he carried was without smell anyway, a scentless Japanese hybrid. Quietly he placed it on the bedspread by her hands and left the room.

A little later the patient awoke to the sound of a terrible commotion in the room. The Matron had been called in, and two other nurses.

'Is this what you call security?' Bar was shouting, 'when complete strangers can walk into these rooms? Isn't it of paramount importance that the patient be left in peace to recover? Just look at this!' She brandished the long-stemmed rose. 'Would you like to tell me how this got in? I turn my back for a minute and this is what happens. I *demand* an explanation.'

But the patient was fully awake now and she had

seen the rose. She smiled.

'Bar,' she said weakly, for she was only just on the road to recovery. 'I believe that flower was intended for me. Would you like to give it to me, please?'

The old man had barely got back to his gate when he was accosted again.

'I say!' said Don, 'I say! I just wanted to give you the good news. I particularly wanted you to be the first to know, because I believe it was you who first pointed me in the right direction. It's Bar!' he said, his eyes lighting up.

'What's Bar?' asked the old man sharply.

'Bar is the one for me. I wasn't so sure, but last night I slept on it, and now I'm sure as sure can be. You see, I always thought it was the other, but how wrong I was! You should see the way the teeny weeny one looks after the other in hospital! It's a sight to behold. I was with her all day today, you see. Next week—*yes, next week!*—I'm going to ask her to marry me. Then she can come live with me on that side of the road. Isn't that *wunnerful*? We'll all be friends together in Surrey Lanka. *Forever*!'

'Let's ask Hitler's mother and Stalin's aunt too,' the old man nearly added. He closed the latch on the gate quickly, before the other could follow him in. 'Congratulations,' he said briefly over his shoulder. Resisting the violent urge to vomit under the mango tree he vanished up the staircase.

24

They must have both overslept because it was late next morning when she shook him awake out of his jet-lagged stupor.

'Stelios didn't come home last night,' she whispered. 'I'm really worried.'

His eyes were glued together. He forced them open and sat up. 'Has he ever done this before?'

'No, never. I'm worried that something may have happened to him at the carnival.'

They got into the GTI and drove to Notting Hill. There were crash barriers pushed to the sides of the roads and debris everywhere from the night before, of what seemed to have been some vast world war.

'Is this what it's always like?' he asked.

'Gets bigger every year,' she said.

They got out of the car and began to walk. Little rickety stands were being set up outside grand Notting Hill mansions: home-made shops selling plantain chips and curry patties and root beer. Big women with muscles were manhandling ten-gallon cauldrons of curry goat and rice-and-peas; the army marched on its stomach and battle was due to commence some time after noon. The magicians of music were setting up their booths at street corners, enormous boxes of sound matt black and baffled.

But no Stelios. They must have asked twenty people if there had been any accidents, any incidents of violence the night before. The answer was always the same: no. Just then she spotted a policeman walking towards them. They went up to him anxiously. 'Officer,' she said. 'I want to report a disappearance. My husband didn't come home last night.'

The policeman's face split into a broad grin. 'We have dozens of complaints like that every year, Miss. It's Carnival. Relax! He'll come home when he's sobered up.'

The crowd was thickening now and the first floats appeared. And suddenly, miraculously, he saw just five yards ahead of him in the surging crowd the Greeks from the Foot Hospital—Elpida and Kalavazides and Zos. 'Hey!' he shouted. '*Hey!*' The music deafened his cries; he pushed his way forward with all his strength.

'Zos!' he yelled and—thank God!—Zos turned round. 'Where's Stelios? Have you seen him?'

Zos looked mildly surprised. 'Of course. He was with us last night. Didn't he get back?'

Kalavazides said something to him in Greek and they laughed. 'Sorry, mate, can't help you, I'm afraid.' The crowd surged around them and they got pulled in different directions. The float that went past just then had three gyrating girls on it, the middle one in short black PVC skirt and no knickers.

'If Stelios is to be found anywhere it'll be here,' Elena said with grim humour. She clutched his arm. 'Let's get out of here before I die of suffocation.'

They struggled against the tide, pushing their way out. It took half an hour before they were clear, and they found themselves under the great concrete structure of the Westway.

'Let's get a drink,' he said, 'no point moping. I'm sure he'll be back.'

It was a struggle to persuade her; finally he virtually had to push her into a pub on All Saints Road. The customers inside were almost a hundred per cent black; the pub sounds died and all eyes were turned on this one white girl. He went up to the bar and got a rum and black for himself, and half a cider for her.

'Cheers,' he said dispiritedly. They drank in silence and the sounds of the pub rose slowly up around them, back to normal levels.

'Be quick,' she said. 'I don't feel so comfortable in here.' He had never known her to be so edgy, and he realized she must really be worried.

He knew where Stelios was, of course. But the rules

of this three-way game were strict, and he was not here to take sides. He remembered Meg's words at the gym that day: *He's promised to take me to the Carnival.* He also remembered her other words. *Never mind, I said. I'll wait.*

All it took was one sentence to destroy their relationship, and perhaps in doing so—just perhaps—it would improve his own chances. But he was not that sort of person. A battle not fought fair and square was no battle at all. Guerrilla tactics were perhaps the modern way of fighting but they were for other people, not him. He was enough his father's son to realize this trait in himself.

As they left, an enormous Rastafarian in little round glasses and knitted red-yellow-and-green cap leant over and patted him on the back: 'Cheer, up man! Surely married life can't be as bad as all that?'

They half hoped that Stelios would be back at the flat when they returned—glass of wine in hand, ready to regale them with tales of the night; but he wasn't. There seemed to be an emptiness now, a space between them they were both aware of, and it made them feel uneasy. They had spent many evenings in his absence before but it had been different, because his impending arrival had always been on their minds, the *presence* of his absence. But that no longer seemed to exist. He wondered how long Meg was going to keep him, how long before good sense prevailed.

He'll never leave me, Elena had said. He remembered how she had also said: 'Your citizenship's not through yet. I can have you sent back at the flick of a hand.' She didn't seem so sure now.

'I'll cook something for you,' he offered, but she shook her head. His resources were depleted, and that was all he could offer her, the only comfort he knew: there was no substitute in his mind for the sheer animal pleasures of food and drink and sex. They opened a bottle of wine and sat down to the long evening ahead, like mourners at a Sri Lankan village wake.

She held her glass up to the light. 'He always thought this was such shit,' she said affectionately. 'But how he gulped it down!'

There was some cheese in the fridge. They ate it as much to pass the time as anything else. It was now past midnight and he took her hand. 'Please,' he said. 'Let's go to bed. Please?' She looked up at him and he could see the significance of what he was suggesting slowly begin to cloud her eyes. She led him to the bedroom.

But inside the bedroom it seemed strange, awkward, just the two of them, and she turned her back on him to undress. Just pretend she's the client and you're the professional, he told himself. You won't feel so nervous then. After all, wasn't that's how it had been, only a few months ago? Silently he slid under the covers and averted his head to spare her any embarrassment. He felt rather than heard her finally get in. She laid a soft tentative hand on his back and he turned towards her; and again he was struck by how compact and beautiful she was, every limb a work of perfection turned and finished on a lathe operated by the gods. She buried her face in his chest and he began kissing her hair, her forehead, her shoulders. His hand began to trace her features, the unbroken line from nose to forehead. They encountered her eyelashes and he realized with a shock they were wet. He sat up on his elbow to look at her.

She was weeping. 'I can't,' she whispered, shaking her head. 'I can't. I love him, you see.' The tears were flowing copiously now and he took her in his arms, gently rocking her back and forth, back and forth, comforting her. And he was flooded anew with love: for her and for that sheer plain goodness that was in her. And he wondered, Would I have had the strength of character to make the same decision if our roles had been reversed?

She went to sleep easily in his arms, her breath rising and falling in a gentle purr; but he stayed awake a long time, looking at the sloping roofs of that small room lit by the faint yellow light coming in through the mansard window. It seemed to him that he had come to a bottleneck in the river. He either had to turn around and swim back against the current; or squeeze through the smallest of gaps with the greatest of difficulty.

So you pick up the phone as you've been meaning to do ever since you got back.

'Gary,' you say, 'it's me, Norton. Remember me?'

'Norton? Course I remember! Welcome back!' Gary chortles. 'I knew you'd be back. Somehow I just knew. You were too good to get away. As it happens I have something for you tonight, a real treat.'

He gives the address, and it's for 8 o'clock, and as you walk past the barbed wire and the industrial yards and the playgrounds you have a strange sense you have been here before, a sort of déjà vu. And you raise your hand to knock on the tiny door of the doll's house and it opens in your face and you realize too late where you are. You are with the Jelly Man.

'I knew you'd be back,' he says echoing Gary. 'I just knew. You darkies, you just can't keep away, can you?' And he locks the door behind you. And you're sick now, just sick with the knowledge of what's going to happen next, so it's almost a relief when he puts his hands round your neck and starts squeezing, and yelling in your face, *Fucker! You fucker! Get up you fucker!* And with a shock you sit up in bed and it's not a dream any more, it's Stelios's hands round your neck, and you realize it's for real and he's within an inch of killing you. And on the other side of the bed you can see Elena crouching in a corner of the room and she's shitting herself too.

'I'm giving you ten minutes,' Stelios says with almost mystic calm now he knows you're up. 'If you're not out of here in ten minutes I will come back and kill you.' And no, he's not joking.

25

His most immediate concern was to see if she was all right.

'Did he hurt you?' he asked softly. She shook her head.

'Come with me,' he said urgently. 'Let's both go. You're not safe with him.'

She looked around the room as if assessing its contents. 'Where would I go?' she asked sadly.

'With me,' he said. 'We can start again somewhere.' He held her more tightly as if to reinforce his convictions. Because at that moment in his life, at that age, anything was possible, everything was possible.

But she was just those few years older, the crucial few years in a person's life when they become suddenly aware of time passing, its finite quality, like so many brightly coloured beads on a circular string you pass through your fingers. She bowed her head, as if all the world's cares were upon her. 'You don't get it, do you,' she said wearily, with a hopeless shake of the head. 'It's him I love. It's always been him.'

Even though he had heard these words the night before, his pride was crushed. There was a pain in his head as if she had taken a fork and raked over the soft internal masses of his brain. And the pain made him see red. Why did you waste my time, then? he wanted to shout. Why did you string me along all these months with your stupid, careless talk of love? *Why did you give me hope?* But he knew only too well that it would be dishonest to claim he had been used. He had got from them just about as much as he had given: not least the power he had exerted over them by being the object of their desire. He knew in matters such as these there was always a bargain struck, a consideration paid; it didn't necessarily have to be about money.

But the anger made him fight on, desperation making him break all rules: because taboos are meant to be broken, aren't they, and what is war after all but a dirty business with a grand-sounding name?

'He's unfaithful to you. I know that for sure. And you know what? The moment he gets his citizenship he's out of here. That's the only thing he's waiting for.' He found himself breathing hard because he knew what he was doing, and it was far worse than mere murder: he was gratuitously killing off someone else's relationship with a viciousness he never knew he had, cutting off its head with a rusty saw.

She didn't say anything. She turned round and unhooked a plastic bag from the dressing table chair. Going to the hall cupboard she began putting his things into it, the dinner jacket, the thin white shirt, the stripey tie.

She stood up on tip-toe and squeezed him hard. 'You have our number. Promise me you'll call? Please?'

But all he could think of was that word *our*. *Our* number.

Chamath walked along Worple Road. Suddenly from nowhere Stelios appeared. Chamath continued walking. Stelios overtook him, turned round and began half walking, half running backwards to keep up with him, like a sort of fitness exercise.

'It's the best thing all round if you go,' he said. His rage was gone: it was almost as if he were trying to persuade himself now of the good sense of his decision. Chamath didn't say anything. He quickened his pace. But still Stelios ran on, backwards, unwilling to let him go. Chamath knew what he wanted. Just those few words from him, *Nothing happened; please forgive me, I'm sorry,* would have been enough for things to go back to how they had been. But Chamath said nothing. He still worshipped his friend. At the same time he thought of his father, the possessor of an immense and foolish pride: he was his father's son in more ways than he cared to admit. He tried to justify himself. I am the rescue dog that is being thrown back out because it tried to bite the hand of the master that fed it. I couldn't help myself, it was in my nature, he thought defiantly. Oh, but how I kept the master's wife happy! They loved me while I was with them, I could do no wrong! But now, like any stray dog, all he could think of was his newfound freedom. I'm out of here, he kept thinking. I'm out of here, I've had enough. He had nowhere to go, no one to turn to. All the same he felt liberated from the chains of his kennel.

After a while he became aware that Stelios was no longer keeping pace with him. He stole a quick look round. He could see Stelios walking back to the flat, head bowed. Chamath walked the last bit of Worple Road alone. You broke the first and only rule of your profession, he told himself severely. You got involved. Don't you realize there is no room in this business for the comfort and self-indulgence of everyday feelings? *You abused your position of power: you got what you deserved.*

Yet as he sat on the District Line, on a return journey to a home he didn't have, the regret and self-pity came flooding back, spreading to the tips of his fingers like ghostly bloodstains on a murderer's hands. *How could they have meant so much to me?* he thought. *How could I have meant so little to them?*

It was always slightly colder in Kensal Green, and there was a breeze on his face as he walked up the gentle slope towards Hiley Road. What a fool! So this was where it had been pointing all along; this was where his future lay. He had forgotten the packet of tea. Just as well I couldn't see her yesterday, he thought. I hope she's cooled down by now.

The door to Jamila's flat was wide open. A man he had never seen before came out. 'Come to repair the door?' he asked. '*Speedy Trades?*'

Chamath shook his head.

The man sat down on the bottom step and put his head in his hands. 'She was still my wife,' he said wearily. 'Divorce hadn't come through yet.'

Wife? Chamath thought in confusion. *Jamila was married?*

The man wore an anorak and glasses. He didn't look like Jamila's type.

'She didn't come round for Gemma yesterday. Takes her to her parents every weekend, you see. But *they* hadn't heard from her either. I called Emergency Services.' His voice broke. 'They had to break the door down.'

It was then that Chamath noticed with shock the cracked door frame, the splinters of door-stop all over the hall floor.

'We were fighting for custody,' the man said. 'I hired the best lawyer money could buy. And she . . .' he shook his head hopelessly, 'she had to settle for legal aid from Immigration Advisory Services.'

Custody? Chamath thought. Gemma? *Who is Gemma?*

And the answer to his question came tripping out of the downstairs flat, a small girl with squeaky shoes. She had a freckled face and masses of curly red hair. She came and nestled against her father. 'Mummy's gone away,' she said to Chamath importantly, as if in answer to a question he had asked. 'She's gone on holiday. We don't know when she'll be back.'

'You can always win if you have the money,' the man said bitterly, 'and I won, you see, big time. I never thought she'd take it so badly.'

There seemed to be a lack of oxygen in the corridor: Chamath was finding it difficult to breathe. Jamila that absolute paragon who, more than anyone else, had stood for all those things he was not and could never be! How could she do this to him? He felt angry and betrayed. And then he felt guilty for being so selfish. Oh Jamila, he thought in panic. Where are you?

'My lawyer was able to persuade court she was unfit to look after Gemma,' the man was saying. 'No proper job, living on council benefits and hand-outs. Whereas I,' he buried his head in his hands and his voice became muffled, 'I had a good job, you see, a decent house, a good area. I was, *am*, in a steady relationship. A nice stable background.'

The man looked up. 'She did say she was in a relationship too. She said it was only a matter of time . . . before she could provide a good environment for the child.'

The man was looking at him now, suspiciously. 'You live upstairs?' he asked.

'Yes,' said Chamath. 'I mean, no.'

'You wouldn't happen to know who this man was, would you? Did *you* know her well?'

And Chamath thought: I have so far betrayed everyone around me, so why stop now? One more won't make any difference.

'No,' he said. 'I hardly knew her. I have *no* idea who this man might have been. I only came here to collect my mail.'

But afterwards, as he sat at the table in the library, the tears came and they would not stop. I was not there for her, he thought. It pained him to think that her simplified code of ethics, her abbreviated vocabulary of rights and wrongs had not been enough to cope in this big city either. What he had thought was the precisely ordered motion of her planet—what he had affected to despise but secretly envied—had been neither as precise nor as ordered as he had imagined. It too had been spinning at the outer edges of the system, till it lost control entirely and extinguished itself. I could have been there for her, he thought, I should have been. How could I not have seen the signals? He was crying now for all these lives around him, all these lives into which he might have fitted so comfortably, as water inside a glass. But you're not responsible for any of them, he told himself, you can't save them all. You are not their keeper: you're not even your father's keeper, remember? The only sure thing is this: that if you choose to go down one particular alley in the maze it only means you have chosen to reject at least three others. Who was to say that if he had chosen to go with Jamila that night she would have been better off? But she would be alive now. She would be alive. There was this small matter of a life. But I didn't love her, he wanted to cry out loud. *I didn't, I didn't!* And she, she never made her feelings clear. On the contrary, she took great pains to show how *little* I meant to her. It wouldn't be the first time he would think: I will never understand women as long as I live: they really are a different race.

'Didn't she get in touch with you?' Constance asked when he called her with news of the suicide. 'She wanted your contact details and I gave her the address in Wimbledon. I hope you didn't mind?'

Had she been trying his number while they were away in Sri Lanka? Was he actually the one she had been looking for that day on Arterberry Road, and been too shy to admit it? 'Looking for a friend,' she had said cryptically, 'couldn't find the address.'

And so he sat there and cried for them all, watched with deep suspicion by the other homeless people at the table, who couldn't understand how anyone could lose their self-respect so shamelessly, in such a public manner. But mostly he cried for himself because he was all alone in the big city with nowhere to go, not even a bed to sleep in that night.

And so you do the only thing possible, the only thing left to you. You go to the telephone box.

Gary, you say, it's me, Norton. Remember me?

And Gary replies, Norton! Of course! And he chortles. You know, somehow I *knew* you'd come back to us? You were too good to get away.

And this time it's no nightmare, it's for real. And he gives you an address, a bed for the night. Because although you have no bed of your own, it seems that there are many people out there in this big city, many, *many* who have one to share. And after all, why should you care? You're good at your job, you have the voice, you have the inches to spare, ha ha. Why should you care if you end up dead in the gutter at thirty?

But mostly you do it because every day when you go into that telephone booth at eleven sharp you have this tiny hope, so small you hardly dare acknowledge it consciously, that Gary or even Mike will say: There's this job in Wimbledon, place called Arterberry Road. They want you there at six this evening. Some woman with a foreign accent.

26

The job was done: the frames of the film re-attached in sequence, the life re-run. The last sheet of paper was still inside the typewriter. The old man took it out and put it carefully with the others, locking up the manuscript in the tin trunk. He sat in his chair and began to dream. Of the intervening thirty-five years. Of the highs and lows of his brilliant career (and no, he had not died by the age of thirty). Of the return of his father's cancer. Of his death.

Constance had found him a room to rent, just round the corner in Bathurst Gardens, almost next door to the library. He spent most mornings there, reading his way through the history of Renaissance Italy, the works of Jalaluddin Rumi and the poetry of his beloved St John of the Cross. The homeless people seated with him at table regarded him with superior disdain—this man who so brazenly dared to disturb the peace by loudly turning pages. Some afternoons he swam before getting ready for the night. He never went to the Clapham gym again.

One morning, coming back from work, he found the thin blue aerogramme lying on his mat, the last letter he was ever to receive from his father. The old gentleman in the train had reached his final destination.

My darling boy,

By the time you get this, I will be no more. Or as Father Mahesh is sure to say at my funeral Mass, *He has gone to a better place*. And when he says this—as I know he surely will!—you have my full permission to laugh out loud in church, secure in the knowledge that I will be laughing up there with you.

I have packed off Sita and Poppy to your aunts' in Kandy. Flower Terrace is already under offer, the sale proceeds to be remitted to your account in London. Yes, there it is: the seed capital for your property development business. You thought I had forgotten, didn't you?

There remains little else for me to say except *bon voyage*, and may you enjoy the rest of *your* journey, as I have mine. It has truly been a pleasure knowing you, my boy! Be well and be good. And

please remember that I have always loved you, to
the best of my somewhat limited ability.

Appachi

And just like that, his whole life changed. It was as if
his father, from 5,000 miles away, had wilfully and
capriciously turned up the colour on his television
set. The old man watched with fascination the fast-
forward scenes of those later years playing out before
his eyes: the dazzling and rather unexpected success of
his conversion business during the Thatcher eighties;
and how finally, against all odds he had cashed in his
chips at the correct time, returning to Sri Lanka just
months before the market crashed in London.

But all the while, even as he watched these dramatic
scenes, brazen and bold, dressed and dancing before
his eyes in lurid Technicolor, the sound on the
television set seemed strangely muted. And in place
of its soundtrack he could hear something else: he
could hear the duck singing merrily on the stove; and
he could smell the spices it was being braised in; as
if that floating honey-coloured kitchen with the matt
black floor were only just behind him.

And he could hear her say softly, 'So where did you
learn to cook?'

There was a commotion below as a pale blue Nano taxicab drove up to the gate, evicting from its interior a pair of quarrelsome landladies.

'Nothing like a hospital stay to improve the complexion, don't you think?' said Bar breathing in the smell of the sea, the odour of ripening mangoes. 'Didn't I look after you well!'

'Did you? I couldn't tell. I was asleep most of the time.'

'Oh, you cheeky monkey. Right, that's it! From now on, strict bed-rest for *at least* a month!'

'A month? Isn't that rather excessive?'

'Is it? I can't have you claiming afterwards I killed you off for the house.'

'I won't be claiming anything by then. I'll be *dead*.' Leaving her suitcase under the mango tree Ginnie began to ascend the steep staircase.

'Good heavens! Where do you think *you're* going?'

'I'm going,' said Ginnie patiently, 'to see a man about a rose.'

'*Dog*, dear. Going to see a man about a *dog*.'

Mention of the word *dog* and the little yard erupted, as Shorts came bounding out of the house to greet his mistresses. But Bar was not about to be side-tracked. 'Ginnie,' she shouted, almost in desperation. '*Get down from that staircase!* It's too soon after hospital to be going to strange places. You might *catch* something up there!'

'I might,' said Ginnie quietly. 'I might catch a man.'

27

A nd this is where I found them, seated on the bed holding hands. I had been happy here once, all those years ago—so this is where he had returned, like a puppy, to dig up that buried bone of happiness: and his story was only just beginning, even if mine had ended all so long ago. I was his past you see, and he my future. By replaying my story, frame by frame, the old man had succeeded in liberating me: I was no longer trapped inside that instant of his memory, embedded in the ordinary cubic dimensions of that world. I was free to walk away. At the same time I could not forget he was my future, and I was curious to see what that future held. So I walked about his little annexe checking out his sparse surroundings with interest—the newspaper under the leaking fridge, the tin of peaches in the cupboard. I noticed he still had my thin white shirt and stripey tie thrown carelessly over the back of the chair, the collar now frayed beyond repair. I wondered what he had done with the prosperous professional clothes of my later years. I didn't see the dinner jacket either, though it was probably around somewhere.

I half hoped the two of them would see me, so I could wish them something of the luck and happiness that had eluded me in my story. But they didn't. *They couldn't*. Their future had just become their present, so their past was well and truly past, trickling away quietly like liquid out of a glass. Still I stood there, silently, looking at them a few more minutes, smiling. I longed to touch them. I knew I couldn't, for our lives are not given to coincide in this physical world as they might do in the pages of a book; or even as they might in the mind of God. So I left as quietly as I had come.

There were no sounds from downstairs, no excited dog, no Fela Kuti. I closed the latch carefully on the gate and began walking down the slope; to the deep and sunlit sea.

Acknowledgements

My heartfelt thanks to Mita Kapur my agent, without whom this novel would never have seen the light of day, my editors Archana Shankar and of course Meru Gokhale, who fearlessly seized the spanner to tighten up the nuts and bolts of this manuscript. Thank you!